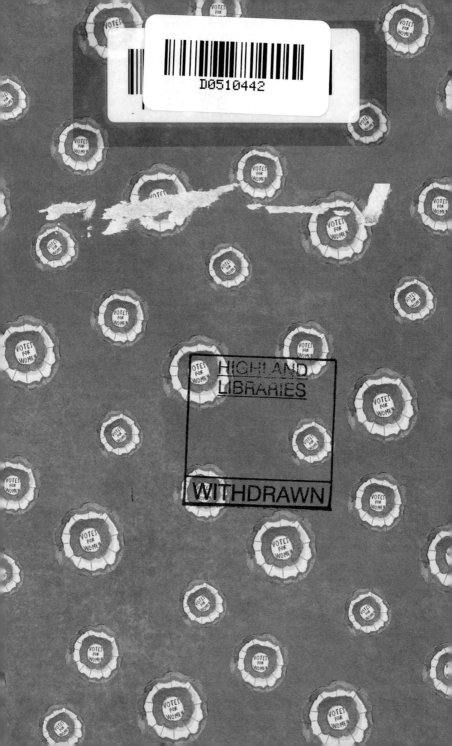

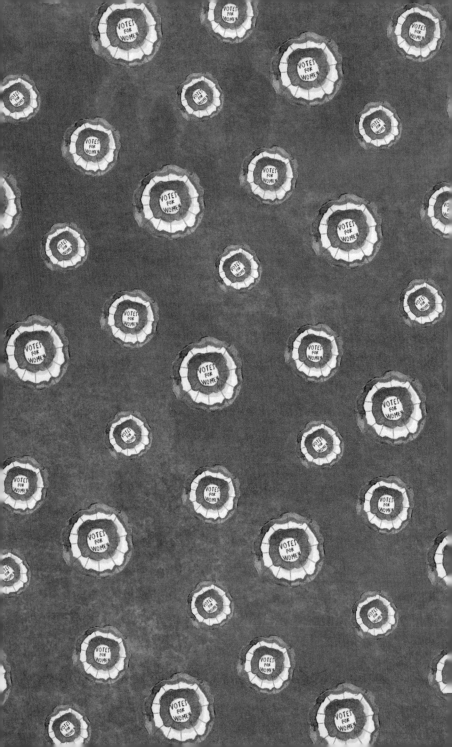

Secret Suffragette

Other books by Barbara Mitchelhill

Billy's Blitz
Dangerous Diamonds
Run Rabbit Run
Storm Runners
A Twist of Fortune

Secret Suffragette

BARBARA MITCHELHILL

First published in the UK in 2019 by
Andersen Press Limited
20 Vauxhall Bridge Road
London SW1V 2SA
www.andersenpress.co.uk

2 4 6 8 10 9 7 5 3 1

British Library Cataloguing in Publication Data available.

ISBN 978 1 78344 833 3

This book is printed on FSC accredited paper from responsible sources

Printed and bound in Great Britain by Clays Ltd, Elcograf S.p.A.

'So this is what I decided: I wouldn't go smashing windows or chaining myself to Buckingham Palace's railings. But I could do something small to start with.'

Daisy O'Doyle

One

That afternoon, it was raining cats and dogs – though I don't know why I say that because there were no cats or dogs to be seen. Just water. Lots of it. Beating down from black clouds and leaving puddles all over the schoolyard.

'Lily!' I yelled as I ran towards the gates. 'Lily, where are you?'

I was late. The schoolyard was empty and there was no sign of my sister. I was supposed to look after her. She was only six.

Dad was always telling me, 'You're twelve now, Daisy. It's up to you to take care of the little ones.'

But here I was, soaking wet and no sign of Lily. Shielding my eyes from the rain and peering around, I shouted 'Lily!' again at the top of my voice.

Suddenly, a head of red curls poked out of the brick building that was the girls' privy. It was Lily. She'd been sheltering from the rain. Very sensible. Good girl.

'I'm here, Daisy,' she called, running across the yard towards me. 'Where've you been? Did Miss Spike keep you in again?'

'Course she did,' I said.

'Why?' she asked as she took hold of my hand.

1

'Because she asked who knew anything about Florence Nightingale. I said I knew everything about her and I stood up and told the class.'

'Why did she keep you in for that?' asked Lily.

'Cos I knew more than she did, that's why.'

Lily giggled and we ran out of the school gates.

'She'd never heard about the Training School for Nurses. So I told her . . .'

We hit a puddle and soaked our boots. But we didn't stop.

'. . . I said I was going to go to that school one day and Miss Spikey-head said I was showing off. She made me write a hundred lines: "I must not be boastful." Oh she's so *stupid*.'

'And you're so *clever*,' said Lily as we ran along the road, laughing. 'Much cleverer than that teacher. And you'll be a nurse one day, won't you, Daisy?'

Luckily, the rain had started to slow down, which meant we could run faster. We were already late to pick up our baby brothers, Eddy and Frank, from Mrs Griggs. She always looked after them while we were at school but she didn't like it if we were late.

Mrs Griggs lived in Tuttle Street like us – backing on to the railway cutting. It wasn't a nice part of Bow. Our street was dark and narrow with houses crammed together on either side. Most days, there were lines of washing strung across from one bedroom window to another. I don't know why people bothered because the soot from the factories dropped black spots everywhere. It was a waste of time, if you ask me.

That day, as we ran up the street, the local girls were sitting on the doorsteps, gossiping as usual, with their baby brothers or sisters on their knees. A few lads were kicking a football over the cobbles.

'Pass it here, Daisy,' Tommy Watkins shouted as the football rolled towards me. So I gave it a sharp kick, sent it bowling back up to him and joined in the game. I loved playing football. It was fun. But Tommy was the only lad who didn't mind me playing with them.

The others shouted, 'Go home, Daisy O'Doyle. Football's for lads,' until Tommy told them to shut up.

It was Jacob Isaacs who caused most of the trouble. 'Think you're a footballer, do yer, carrot-top?' he yelled as he dribbled the ball towards me. Showing off, he was. Dribble. Dribble. Dribble. Then . . . *bang!* I toed the ball out of his way. It was a brilliant kick! But Jacob was fuming and he gave me a swift shove on the shoulder, pushing me on to the wet stones. *Wham!* I fell flat on my face, which made the boys laugh. Not one of them helped me up. They just carried on with their game while I struggled to my feet. What a mess I was in! There was a hole in my pinafore and it was covered in mud. My knees were badly grazed and two buttons had burst off my right boot. Mum wouldn't be pleased.

'Quick! Get up, Daisy,' said Lily, holding out her hand. 'We'll be late and we don't want Mrs Griggs to shout at us, do we?'

I limped to the top of Tuttle Street where Mrs Griggs lived.

Even from outside the door, you could hear the sound of babies crying. Lots of them. She must be looking after dozens.

'Go on, Lily. You knock,' I said.

While I rubbed the grazes on my knees, Lily kept tapping her little fist on the door until it was flung open. Mrs Griggs stood there, her angry face flushed and sweaty. She was holding Eddy in one arm and Frank in the other.

'Where've you been?' she snapped. 'Messing about with the lads, was yer? You're late!'

'Very sorry, Mrs Griggs. My teacher wanted me to help her after school,' I lied. 'I couldn't say no, could I?'

Mrs Griggs glared at me and sniffed, obviously not believing a word.

'You're always late, Daisy O'Doyle,' she said. 'So you can tell your mother that when you bring the twins tomorrow, I'll be charging a penny extra.' Then she leaned forward and thrust the babies at us.

'Another penny?' I gasped as I grabbed hold of Eddy and Lily took Frank. 'What? Every day?'

Mrs Griggs screwed up her face and folded her arms

over her chest. 'If your mum don't like it, she can find somebody else to look after 'em. I'm not working for nothin'.'

And with that she slammed the door in our faces.

Two

Lily and I hurried home to number 34, carrying the twins. We lived in two rooms rented from Mrs Rosen, who lived upstairs with her six kids.

The front room was where Mum cooked when we had coal for a fire. There was a table with two chairs and a colourful rag rug on the floor that Mum had made years ago out of bits of cloth. The back room was the bedroom where we all slept. Eddy and Frank had a box on the floor. Mum, Dad, Lily and me had the bed.

When we reached our house, Alice Rosen – who was the same age as me – was sitting on the front doorstep minding her baby brother, George.

'You're late home, ain't yer?' she said. 'I bet Mrs Griggs gave you a piece of her mind.'

I didn't want to stop and chat to that nosey so-and-so. 'Got to get inside quick,' I said as I pushed past her. 'The babies need feeding.'

Once we were in our front room, we put the boys on the rug in front of the grate where they wriggled and started to wail.

'I'll make some bread and milk,' I said to Lily. 'You

keep your eye on 'em. Eddy's going to be crawling before we know it.'

I took a loaf of bread out of the bin, ready to cut into chunks.

'Daisy,' said Lily, pinching her nose. 'The twins smell bad. They must be dirty.'

I put the knife down and sighed. I couldn't deny it, there was a horrible stink. 'I suppose we'd better clean 'em up before we feed 'em, eh?'

Lily pulled a face. 'I suppose so. Why doesn't Mrs Griggs ever do it?'

It was what I dreaded most – cleaning the babies' bottoms at the end of the day. But I told myself that Florence Nightingale wouldn't make a fuss about such a thing. She'd just get on with it.

I pulled the water bucket from under the table but it was empty.

'Go to the water pump while I undress the boys, Lily.'

She nodded, picked up the bucket and ran out of the house. She was probably glad to get away from the smell. The water pump was only at the bottom of the street so she was back with the water in no time.

'There wasn't much of a queue,' she said. 'Just Mrs Pidgeon from the end house. You know what she asked me, Daisy?'

'What?'

'She asked if I was big enough to carry a bucket of water. But I told her I'm six now.'

'That's right, Lily. You tell her! You're a big girl.'

I won't describe what it was like to clean up Eddy and Frank. They screamed the place down as if they were being murdered or something. I don't think they liked cold water much.

First we washed them and then we wrapped them in pieces of clean cloth. After that, we fed them the bread and milk. It would have been nice if we could have warmed it but the fire wasn't lit so we couldn't put the pan on. Anyway, they must have been hungry because they ate it just the same. Then we carried them into the bedroom and tucked them into the box Dad had made specially and they soon fell asleep.

Lily watched as I cut two slices of bread for us. 'Daisy, can we have some fish paste on it? I'm starving.'

Great-Aunt Maude had given us a small jar only last week and there was a little bit left in the bottom, so I spread that in a thin layer over the bread. Oh, it was so good.

We had hardly finished eating when one of the lads came tapping on the window. It was Tommy Watkins.

'Daisy!' he shouted. 'Me and the others are off to the jam factory. Do you want to come? Joe says there's something going on down there.'

I pushed up the window and stuck my head out. 'What's happening?' I asked.

'Don't you know?' he said.

'If I did know, Tommy Watkins, I wouldn't be asking you, would I?'

He grinned. 'Well, some posh ladies have come here from up west and they're talking about votes for women.'

'Votes?' I said. 'What are votes?'

Tommy just laughed.

Then Jacob Isaacs joined in. 'They're called suffragettes,' he said, with a sneer in his voice. 'They think women should be equal to men. Well, I ask you, how can they be? Men's brains are bigger. Everybody knows that. If the police get wind of what they're up to, they'll be there in a flash and they'll cart 'em off.'

'Well, it doesn't sound like much fun to me,' I said. 'No, I don't want to come.' And I slammed the window shut.

Three

Dad was back from work. 'Where are my favourite girls?' he called as he burst through the front door.

'We're here, Dad,' shouted Lily, laughing and flinging her arms round his waist.

Mum came in behind, looking tired. 'Are the boys all right?' she asked and gave us both a kiss on the cheek. I told her they were fast asleep and she said, 'Good girl, Daisy.'

Dad took off his cap and tossed it on to the hook before he flopped in his chair. 'Light the fire and make us a cuppa, will you, Florrie?' he said to Mum. Then he winked at me and tickled Lily to make her giggle.

'There's not much coal, Patrick,' said Mum.

Dad peered in the coal scuttle. 'There's enough,' he said.

'But there's no water,' said Mum. 'Daisy, will you fetch some, please?'

'Righto,' I said and I reached under the table for the bucket. It was empty again, I knew.

Dad settled down to light his pipe.

While I was at the pump getting the water, Tommy Watkins and the lads came round the corner.

'How was it at the jam factory?' I asked.

'You should have been there, Daisy,' said Tommy. 'There were these two ladies – suffragettes – dressed up to the nines with posh hats and gloves and whatnot. They were giving out these bits of paper called handbills when the workers came out of the factory.'

'What for?' I asked.

'Think they're to tell people to come to their meetings,' said Tommy. 'But that won't do much good! Most workers can't read.'

'Yeah,' Jacob Isaacs blurted out. 'And they were calling "Votes for women!" all la-di-da. And some of the men called out "Why aren't you at home making your husband's dinner?"'

'It weren't half a laugh,' said one of the other lads. 'Somebody threw a mud ball and hit one of 'em square on the jaw.'

I pretended to laugh but inside I felt a bit sorry for the lady.

'By the way,' said Jacob, 'your friend Eliza was there. She works at the jam factory now, don't she?'

I nodded. She was my best friend and I'd missed her since she'd left school. Now I wished I'd gone with the boys.

'She said to tell you she'll meet you in the park on Sunday.'

By this time, the bucket was full. 'Thanks. I've got to go now.'

'I'll carry that,' said Tommy.

Even though I could carry it myself, I thought it was kind of him.

'The suffragettes are at the shirt factory tomorrow, I heard,' he said as we walked up our street.

'We'll definitely be going,' said Jacob. 'We ain't had any excitement in Bow for a long time.'

'Will you come, Daisy?' Tommy asked.

By then we'd reached our front door. 'I might,' I said, taking hold of the bucket. 'I'll have to see.'

Mum had already lit the fire and the room was beginning to warm up. She filled the kettle with the water and put it on the fire to boil.

'I've just seen Tommy Watkins,' I said. 'They went to see some ladies called suffragettes outside the jam factory. They were handing out handbills or something.'

'Suffragettes?' said Dad, drawing on his pipe. 'They're just posh women with too much time on their hands, ain't they, Florrie? That lot in Parliament won't even let men like *me* vote, so you women have got no chance.' And he winked at Mum. I didn't really understand what they were talking about, but she didn't look convinced.

'Did Eddy and Frank behave themselves for Mrs Griggs today?' Mum asked, changing the subject.

'Mrs Griggs was ever so cross,' said Lily.

'Yes! She was in a right bad mood,' I said, not mentioning the fact that we'd been late to collect them. 'She said to tell you that if she's going to carry on looking after the twins, she wants another penny a day.'

My last words fell like a blow on Mum. 'What?' she said, her eyes wide open. 'Another penny?' She looked at Dad, horrified. 'How are we going to find that, Patrick? We can barely manage as it is.'

We didn't have much money these days – but it hadn't always been like that. Three years before, Dad had worked as a stevedore on the docks. The strongest man for miles around, he was. We lived in a nicer house then, not far from the docks. We had our own front door and a bedroom upstairs. But Dad had a bad accident unloading a ship. A crate fell on him and broke his leg. It was awful. He couldn't work for ages and we had to move to Tuttle Street because the rent was cheaper. After that, Dad always walked with a limp and he couldn't do such hard work. He got a job at the shirt factory and so did Mum, but the money wasn't good. An extra penny a day to look after the boys . . . well, that would be hard to find.

For a few minutes, there was a horrible silence. The only noise came from upstairs where the Rosen kids were running about.

Eventually, Dad said, 'Well, there's one way we could solve our problems.'

'How?' asked Mum.

Dad rubbed his chin. 'Our Daisy could leave school.'

Mum looked at him sharply and I glanced in surprise at Lily.

'She could look after the twins,' Dad continued, 'so we wouldn't have to pay Annie Griggs, for one thing.

13

And she might be able to do a bit of work at home. There's a bloke at the factory and his girl gets six shillings for gutting twenty-four rabbits. Think what we could do with that sort of money.'

Mum listened to Dad but I could tell she wasn't happy with what he'd said.

Finally, she spoke. 'Back in Ireland, Patrick, I worked from the time I could walk. There was hardly a moment to rest. I had little to no schooling, as you well know – and neither did you.'

Dad frowned but he didn't say anything.

'When we grew up,' Mum continued, 'you and me decided to come to England so we could raise a family and give them the things we never had – like a decent education.'

'Ah, them was just airy-fairy dreams . . .'

'But isn't that what you want for your children, Patrick? Daisy's bright as a button. She should stay at school for at least another year. Maybe then she can do more with her life.'

'Florrie,' said Dad, shaking his head. 'An education's not important for a girl, is it? She's only going to get married and have kids. She's had enough schooling. Plenty of girls start work at her age. Some a lot sooner.'

'Oh yes,' Mum replied. 'And if she leaves, the school attendance officer will be round, for sure.'

Dad laughed. 'Who's ever seen an attendance officer round here? Most of the kids in the street don't go to school. Half of 'em are working and the other half are staying at home looking after the babies in the family.'

'Is that the life you want for Daisy?' Mum asked.

Dad didn't answer and Mum turned to look at me. 'What do you think, Daisy? Do you want to leave school?'

'No,' I said. 'I want to be a nurse. You know I do.'

Mum nodded and patted my hand.

'You've heard of Florence Nightingale, haven't you, Dad?' I asked.

'Aye. I know the name,' he said, drawing on his pipe. 'She was from a posh family, I think.'

'But she set up a training school for girls like me. I really want to go there when I'm old enough. Please, Dad.'

He sighed and wiped his forehead. 'That's just another dream, Daisy. People like us don't go to places like that.'

'But Dad . . .'

His face clouded over and he looked sad. 'We're practically facing the workhouse, Daisy. What do you expect me to say?'

I knew Mum was on my side. But silence fell. Mum's shoulders slumped and she said, 'There's four pennies in the jar, Patrick. That'll pay Mrs Griggs the extra till the end of the week. Then we'll just have to think of something.' She looked sad and defeated. 'You'd better go to bed, girls. Daisy, give me your pinafore. I need to brush the mud off it and it needs patching. You can't go to school with a great hole like that in it.'

I gave Mum the pinafore before Lily and I went into the bedroom. The twins were sleeping soundly in their box and we spoke in whispers as we undressed so we didn't wake them up.

We climbed into the big bed – Mum and Dad slept at the top, Lily and me at the bottom. But that night I didn't fall asleep straight away. I kept thinking about what Dad had said. I was scared he'd decided on my future. But it wasn't fair. Shouldn't I have a say in it? I didn't want to be a childminder or work in a factory six days a week. I wanted to be a nurse. Helping sick people – just like Florence Nightingale. She was really famous and Mum was named after her. Ever since I was little, Mum had told me stories about her and how she helped injured soldiers in the war. She was ever so brave and clever too. I wanted to be like her.

I squeezed my eyes tight shut. 'Please let me stay at school, Dad,' I said under my breath. 'Please, please, please. I'll be good. I'll work hard and I'll even be nice to Miss Spike. I promise.'

As I lay there, I wondered if the suffragettes would have anything to say about girls like me. I didn't know about votes or anything like that, but I knew that things weren't fair for girls around here. Maybe I'd go with Tommy tomorrow and find out.

Four

The next day, when we'd finished giving the twins their tea, Tommy Watkins came knocking on the window.

'We're off to see the suffragettes again. Are you coming, Daisy?' he shouted through the glass.

I knew I wanted to go. The lads were just going for a laugh, but I was keen to see for myself what the suffragettes were all about.

'Wait a minute,' I called back to him. 'I'll see if Lily wants to come – but then we'll have to bring the babies.'

I could hear Jacob Isaacs moaning and groaning. 'Come on, Tommy. Let's go. We don't want girls with us anyway.'

I asked Lily if she'd like to come but she shook her head. 'Not with them lads, Daisy.'

'Oh, come on, Lily, I'm dying to find out what's happening!'

'No! I want to stay at home. Can I?'

I knew the boys would leave if I didn't hurry. So I ran upstairs where Mrs Rosen was sitting patching some trousers.

'Mrs Rosen,' I said. 'Could you please keep an eye on Lily and the boys for a bit? I'll be back in half an hour.'

She glanced up at me and I thought how tired she looked. But she managed to smile and said, 'Don't you worry, my lovely. I'll pop down when I've finished these trousers.'

'Thank you,' I called as I ran back downstairs and told Lily.

She grinned. 'I'll go and sit on the step for a bit with Alice and the other big girls.'

'Right then,' I said. 'And Mrs Rosen will come down soon to see you're all right.'

Lily nodded. 'You go, Daisy. I'll be good.'

I slipped out through the front door and pushed past Alice Rosen on the step.

'Where are you off to?' she asked.

'Just out,' I said.

'You're going off with the lads to see them crazy ladies, ain't yer?' she said. 'I'll tell your mum!'

She was only jealous because I was having a bit of fun and she hadn't been invited. The boys were standing there waiting for me. Jacob Isaacs looked really annoyed at being kept waiting and he shouted, 'Come on, if you're coming!'

The shirt factory was a large brick building in Ordell Road – about ten minutes' walk away. I knew all about it because it was where Mum and Dad worked.

When we finally reached it, I saw four ladies by the factory gates – all dressed ever so smart with big hats and everything. One of them was talking to a local woman who had walked up to the gates to see what was going on. She was trying to give her a piece of paper, which I realised must be a handbill.

'Please, take this,' the posh lady said. 'You can read all about the meeting, my dear. It's most important.'

'Don't want no readin', missus,' said the woman and pushed the handbill back, then folded her arms across her chest and glared. 'I'm waiting for me husband to come out of work. What are you doing, wasting your time standing about? We don't want your sort round here.'

'But we're here to help,' said the lady. 'Women must stand together and demand equal rights to men. Why should you not be paid the same as your husband, simply because you are a woman? Why is it men who run the country? Are our brains not equal to men's? Are our rights not as important?'

'Well, I don't know about that,' said the woman. 'All I know is that getting the vote won't help women like me. A vote won't put money in my pocket and food in my belly, will it?'

'But don't you see—' started the suffragette, and I craned forward to hear how she would answer that. But just then the factory siren sounded and a great flood of workers came pouring out of the gates.

The suffragettes started waving their handbills and shouting, 'Votes for women! Don't leave it to the men to make our laws. Come to our meeting and learn about our cause.'

A lot of the workers started jeering and shouting at them. Men called out some horrible names and some of the women shouted awful things too.

'You don't belong here, missus.'

'We don't need the likes of you!'

'Get away with you!'

One of the suffragettes caught hold of the arm of a woman worker before she could stride past. 'Please take a handbill,' she said, pushing the paper into her hand. 'It'll tell you all about our meeting. I'm sure you'll benefit from coming along. It will be most interesting. This cause is for *all* women.'

The woman went red in the face, shook her arm free and raised her clenched fist. 'Shut yer cakehole,' she said and screwed up the paper, stuffing it into the suffragette's mouth. Then she strode away.

It was really embarrassing. People were bent double, laughing at the suffragette – but I didn't think it was funny. I felt really sorry for her. She was only trying to give out a handbill, after all.

I'd have run a mile if somebody shouted such awful things to me. But the posh ladies didn't. They stood their ground and kept talking about votes and equal rights. I really didn't understand. What was so important about a vote that the suffragettes would put up with people shouting at them and catcalling? They must be mad if they thought that women would ever be treated like men – although I wished they could be.

By now, Tommy and the lads had moved forward, nearer to the action. Jacob Isaacs was bending down, picking up stones and dropping them into his pocket. I knew he was up to no good.

'Hey! Jacob!' I shouted. 'What are you doing?'

'Just wait, Daisy O'Doyle,' he said, 'and you might see some fun.'

Then he straightened up and flung a stone at a suffragette. I was shocked, I can tell you! But luckily he had a rotten aim and it missed her.

When he reached into his pocket for another stone I ran towards him, shouting, 'Stop it! You can't do that!'

But I was too late and he flung a second stone in the same direction. This time it was on target. It hit the suffragette's forehead and she staggered backwards. Her hat flew off and landed in the crowd.

Some of them cheered – but, like me, some didn't think it was right. That stone could have put her eye out.

Even so, one of the men shouted, 'Good shot, lad!' and another held up the hat and waved it in the air, crumpled and covered in dirt.

As I watched that poor lady trying to keep her dignity, tears pricked my eyes. I was glad that Lily wasn't with me. She'd have hated every minute. The workers were pushing and jostling the suffragettes. It was turning into a riot.

Jacob was getting ready to throw another stone when somebody suddenly shouted, 'Jacob Isaacs!'

I looked in the direction of the voice and saw Mum marching towards him, looking furious.

'Now go straight home, my lad, or your father will hear about this,' she said, standing in front of him and wagging her finger in a very threatening manner. 'I don't suppose he'll be very pleased to hear that his son has been throwing stones at women. What were you thinking of? It's a good thing the coppers weren't here, that's all I can say, or they could have marched you off to the police station.'

Jacob dropped the stone and slunk away. Then Mum noticed me and Tommy. 'Daisy!' she said. 'How come you're here? And where's Lily and the boys?'

'Mrs Rosen's keeping an eye on 'em,' I said.

'We didn't come to make trouble, Mrs O'Doyle,' said Tommy. 'We just came to hear what the suffragettes had to say.'

'Well,' said Mum. 'As you can see, they're not getting much of a chance to say anything, Tommy, so I suggest you go home.' Tommy scarpered as quick as you like.

Mum turned to me, still looking cross. 'You wait here, Daisy,' she said. 'I'm going to see if those ladies are all right. Disgraceful behaviour.'

The crowd around the gates was thinning by then and I watched Mum go over to the suffragette who had lost her hat and they stood there talking for quite a while. I saw the lady pass Mum a handbill, which she put in her pocket.

As the last of the men workers walked through the gates, I suddenly spotted Dad. He was taller than most of the men and was easy to see with his ginger hair. I waved and ran over to him.

'What are you doing here, Daisy girl?' he asked, ruffling my hair.

'I came to see the suffragettes, Dad.'

'Did you?' he said. 'Well, from what I could see, they just like making a lot of noise and causing trouble. Have you seen your mum?'

'She's over there,' I said, 'talking to that suffragette.'

But Mum had already seen Dad and she was walking towards us.

'This is a nice surprise, isn't it, Patrick?' she said, taking his arm.

'Surprise? You mean them women with their silly bits of paper?'

'No! I mean Daisy being here to meet us. We'll be able to walk home together.'

And so we did, and we chatted happily, as if last night's argument had never happened – and Mum never mentioned the handbill she'd been given.

Five

As we walked home, Mum said she'd get some bread and potatoes from the corner shop. 'I'm hoping Mrs Kaylock will have a drop of milk left too,' she said. 'Run home, Daisy, and fetch the jug, will you?'

Dad looked worried. 'How are you going to pay for it, Florrie? We need that money in the pot for Mrs Griggs.'

Mum smiled. 'Sure, Mrs Kaylock will put it on the slate. She knows I get paid tomorrow.'

'Well, all right,' said Dad. 'But don't go spending like a wild thing. Be careful.'

I was back with the jug in no time. Mum bought a loaf which was yesterday's – stale but cheap – and three potatoes, an onion and half a jug of milk.

She looked pleased. 'Now I shall make some potato soup and we'll have a grand supper,' she said.

'We'll need a fire,' said Dad. 'Lucky I picked up some bits of wood from the factory yard this afternoon, eh?' And I saw that Dad's pockets were bulging. My dad was clever in lots of ways.

Lily was not sitting on the front step when we got home. As we opened the front door, she flung herself at Dad. 'I've been looking after Eddy and Frank all by myself,' she said. 'We sat outside for a bit and then I put them to bed cos they was cryin'. Mrs Rosen said I was a good girl.'

'You certainly are, Lily,' said Dad, picking her up and twirling her round. 'You're quite the little lady now, aren't you? Let's go and see the boys.'

We all peeped into the bedroom where the twins were curled up, still fast asleep.

With the wood Dad had brought, Mum lit the fire and added the few lumps of coal that were left in the scuttle. Then she chopped the potatoes and the onion and put them in the pan with some water from the bucket. Once the fire was hot and the pan was set on top of it, it wasn't long before the smell of the soup filled the room and made my mouth water. I loved potato soup. I liked dipping my bread in it because it made it go nice and soft. Delicious!

When we'd all finished, Dad lit his pipe and Mum pulled a handbill out of her pocket, unfolded it and smoothed it out on the table.

'This is what the suffragette ladies were handing out,' she said to Dad. 'So I thought I'd have one. See what it's all about.'

'What do you want that for, Florrie?' he asked, wrinkling his brow. 'Them suffragettes is just causing trouble. Everybody at the factory says so. You saw what happened at the gates.'

Mum pretended not to hear. 'Daisy,' she said. 'Read it out, will you, love?'

Neither Mum nor Dad could read very well. I knew that but they didn't like anybody else knowing.

I picked up the handbill. 'It says:

Bow Baths Hall.

Sunday 2.00

Free entry.

Speakers will talk about

Better education,

Better working conditions

And votes for women.

All welcome.'

I put the handbill back on the table.

'That sounds interesting, don't you think, Patrick?' Mum said. 'I'd like to go and see what they have to say.'

Dad frowned again.

'Haven't you got enough to do, Florrie?' he said. 'There's the kids to look after and this place needs cleaning. Why do you want to go wasting your time listening to them women? I look after us well enough, don't I?'

'Patrick,' Mum said calmly as she returned the handbill to her pocket, 'I am not complaining about you. But surely you're all for better working conditions and better education, aren't you?'

Dad gave a sort-of grunt as if he didn't like what Mum was saying.

'Sunday is the only day I'm not at the shirt factory,' she continued. 'Every other day I work from seven in the morning to seven at night. I'm thinking it would be nice to do something different for an hour or two, and think about how life could be different for us and for our children.'

'Different?' Dad said, raising his voice. 'You're my wife and I don't want you to do something different! I don't want you mixing with them la-di-da suffragettes. They're not for the likes of us, Florrie. They're troublemakers putting silly ideas in women's heads.'

'You mean like votes for women? Is that silly, Patrick?'

'YES!' he shouted. 'I haven't got no vote and the men I work with haven't either – so why should you women be any different?'

'That doesn't make it right!' Mum snapped. 'Anyway, it's more than just voting. It's like Daisy said – "better working conditions". That would help all of us, wouldn't it?'

He took a deep breath. 'I'll have no more arguing, Florrie. You're not going to the meeting – and that's that.'

'Why not?' said Mum. 'Why shouldn't I go?'

'Because I said you can't and I'm the head of this house.'

'Well, it's talk like that what makes me want to hear what the suffragettes have to say. I don't see what's wrong with going to listen to intelligent women talking.'

Dad pushed back his chair and stood up. 'I've had enough of your prattling, woman,' he said. 'I'm going out.' And he marched through the front door, slamming it behind him.

I looked across at Lily. 'Why's Dad angry?' she sobbed as tears spilled down her face. 'Where's he gone?'

Mum wrapped her arms round her. 'Don't worry yourself, Lily,' she said, wiping Lily's cheeks with her apron. 'He'll be back before you know it. You know your dad doesn't mean half the things he says.'

While we cleared the bowls from the table and washed them in the water bucket, Mum fetched her sewing box off the shelf.

'I must lengthen that dress of yours, Daisy,' she said. 'How did you get to be so tall? I've never known a girl grow so fast!'

'I know, Mum,' I said. 'But I can't help it.'

Mum laughed. 'You've only had that dress for a year or so and it barely covers your knees. Take it off, please, and I'll see what I can do.'

Mum was clever with a needle and thread. She found a piece of material in her sewing bag – it was a lovely shade of purple – and she stitched a wide strip on to the bottom of the skirt. Her stitches were so neat you'd never guess that the purple trimming hadn't been there all the time.

'That looks lovely, Mum,' I said when I put the dress back on. 'Thank you.' I gave her a hug and then

I whispered into her ear, 'Are you going to go to the suffragette meeting on Sunday?'

'I think I just might,' she said. 'And you can come too, if you like, Daisy. I reckon you're old enough, and things need to change around here.'

My heart was suddenly racing. A suffragette meeting! Oh yes, I wanted to go more than anything. Better education, they'd said. Might they find a way for me to stay at school? I couldn't wait to find out.

'I'd really like to, Mum,' I replied.

'Good. But don't tell your father,' she said and tapped the side of her nose. 'Let's keep it our secret.'

Six

Every Sunday morning, Dad would go over to Great-Aunt Maude (who lived not far away) and take her to Mass. Lily and I used to go with them but we were supposed to sit still and listen to the priest talk for ages and ages. Lily found it impossible – and so did I most of the time – which made Great-Aunt Maude really angry. So Dad stopped taking us.

Mum never went to Mass now. Not since our little brother, Archie, died. I don't know why. Instead, she took us to Victoria Park where we could run around as much as we wanted. There was an old stone shelter where Mum liked to sit while we played. Every time we went there, she would point to the words carved above the wooden bench.

'Read that out loud, Daisy,' she'd say. 'I want you to remember it.'

So I'd stand there and, in my best and loudest voice, I'd read what it said: 'This alcove which once stood on old London Bridge, was presented to Her Majesty by Benjamin Dixon Esquire.'

'You see, this shelter is very, very old,' she'd explain. 'Yet, after all these years, its stone walls and its lovely curved roof still protect us from the wind and rain. Don't you think that's wonderful?'

And every time, we'd laugh and say, 'Yes, Mum,' before running off to throw pebbles into the bathing pool, while she sat in the shelter happily bouncing the twins on her knees until Lily and I came back.

Going to Victoria Park was our treat and we loved it. That Sunday morning I was looking forward to seeing Eliza there too. But we were surprised when, just before we left the house, Mum said she wasn't coming with us.

'You and Lily can go by yourselves,' she said. 'I'd better stay at home and clean up a bit. I need to keep on the right side of your father.'

We groaned with disappointment because that meant we'd be in charge of the twins. Mum wagged her finger at us. 'No moaning now. And when you come back, there'll be a surprise.'

'What? What is it, Mum?' we asked. 'Please tell us now.'

'We're having ox cheek for dinner,' she smiled.

'Ox cheek? Really?' I was hardly able to believe it. We almost never had meat.

Mum nodded. 'I got it from the butcher yesterday when I got paid.'

'My favourite!' said Lily. And she flung herself at Mum, wrapping her arms round her waist.

Mum laughed. 'Get away with you, and make sure you're not late back.'

As if we'd miss a meat dinner! I don't think so.

We headed for the front door but before I stepped on to the street, I turned and looked back at Mum. She nodded and winked at me, and I knew what that meant. She still intended to go to the suffragette meeting that afternoon.

When we reached Victoria Park, Eliza was already waiting in the shelter. As soon as she saw us she jumped up, waving like mad.

'I knew it was you two,' she said when we got near. 'I could see that red hair of yours a mile away.'

We sat down in the shelter and I said, 'I ain't half missed you, Eliza. School's just not the same without you.'

'I miss you too,' said Eliza. 'And can you believe it, I actually miss school.'

I was shocked to hear her say that. She had never really liked school. Not like me. She wasn't that good at lessons and she'd been excited about leaving and earning money.

'But I thought you wanted to work at the jam factory?' I said.

Before Eliza could answer, Lily started tugging my sleeve. 'I don't want to stay here, Daisy,' she said. 'I want to go down to the lake. Can I?'

'All right,' I said. 'But you're not to go in the water. Promise?'

'I promise,' she said and ran off straight away to watch some boys laughing as they splashed each other.

We set the twins down on the grass where they

rolled around happily, leaving Eliza and me to have a good long chat. 'Go on then,' I said. 'Tell me all about it.'

'Oh, Daisy,' she sighed. 'I know I never liked lessons. I just wanted to leave school and earn some money. But the jam factory isn't what I thought it would be. For a start, the men keep shouting silly remarks and pinching me. They think it's funny but it isn't. It's so embarrassing and I hate walking past 'em.'

'That sounds awful,' I replied. 'Jacob Isaacs will be just like that when he's grown up – that's for sure. He's a real pain already. He thinks he's much cleverer than us girls. But he's not.' Then I pulled a face and we both laughed. 'But never mind the men. What about the work? What do you have to do?'

'Well, us youngest girls have to wash the jam pots. It sounds easy, but heavens, it's such dirty work, Daisy.' She held out her hands and I couldn't believe the big scars across her palms. 'We're always getting cut, see, but it ain't easy working with rags on our hands and we get told off if we slow down.'

I took hold of her hand and stroked it. 'Oh poor you, Eliza. How terrible.'

'That ain't half of it. Our skirts and ankles get soaking wet from standing in pools of water all day. They give us clogs for our feet but they don't fit so good and the water still gets inside.'

By then tears had welled up in her eyes and I put my arm round her.

'You get paid, at least, don't you?' I said. 'Money of your very own! I can't even imagine. What will you buy?'

But even that didn't cheer her up.

'I got paid yesterday,' she sobbed. 'Two shillings, Daisy. Two shillings cos I was still learning, they said. And I was slow. But I'd worked six days for that. Four pennies a day! It's just not right.'

'I know,' I said. 'I'm sure you'll get faster, though.'

'Maybe, but then I'll just get pieces of glass in my hand or I'll slip on the wet stones,' she said, burying her face in her hands. 'Honest, Daisy, if it wasn't for the other girls, I couldn't do it, day after day. They're the only good thing about the place. At least we have a laugh sometimes.'

I looked up to see Lily running towards us, her red hair blowing wild in the wind.

'I'd better go,' said Eliza. 'I've got to help Mum make matchboxes. She's got behind this week.'

She stood up and so did I.

'Whatever you do, Daisy, stay at school for as long as you can. You can do better than me. You're clever, you are.'

Looking tired and sad, Eliza turned and headed towards home. I felt so sorry for her but, after what she'd told me, I was more certain than ever that I wouldn't work in a factory. *EVER!* I was going to be a nurse like Florence Nightingale.

Seven

We hurried home from the park in time for dinner and when we opened the front door, the smell of the ox cheek bubbling away in the pan was heaven!

'Is it ready, Mum?' asked Lily, running up to the table. We were both looking forward to the taste of meat and even the twins were looking excited.

Dad was back from Great-Aunt Maude's and was sitting in his chair waiting for his dinner.

'It smells grand, don't it, Lily?' he said and pulled her on to his knee.

Mum cut some bread into slices and put them on the table. Then she took the pan off the fire and ladled the ox-cheek stew into bowls. Lily and me stood at the end of the table between Mum and Dad, dipping our bread into the thick brown gravy. I closed my eyes and held it in my mouth. What a taste! It was *beautiful . . . delicious.* The best dinner I'd ever had.

It was a shame that, just when we were eating, the Rosen kids upstairs started jumping about and plaster from the ceiling started dropping on to the table.

'It's like a snowstorm,' said Dad as we all lifted our bowls out of the way and held them in our hands until the shower stopped. But even that didn't spoil our meal.

When we'd finished and cleaned our bowls with the last bit of bread, Dad said, 'That was very tasty, Florrie.' Then he wiped his mouth on his shirtsleeve and stood up. 'Now I'm going over to see Tom. He's wanting to borrow a hammer to fix his front door.'

Tom worked with Dad at the shirt factory. They were best friends and often helped each other out.

'Will you be back late?' asked Mum.

Dad grinned. 'Maybe Tom'll treat me to a pint when the Gunmaker's Arms opens again. So I might be late.'

Mum nodded. He'd obviously forgotten about the suffragette meeting or didn't believe Mum would ever go.

Mum didn't say a thing as Dad went out, but once he'd gone, she stood up and said, 'Clear the table quickly, girls, while I go up to see Mrs Rosen. We've just got time to get to that meeting.'

I nodded. I was really excited.

'Can I look after Eddy and Frank?' asked Lily when Mum came back. 'I don't really want to go to no meeting, Mum.'

'Of course you can, darlin',' said Mum. 'I've asked Mrs Rosen to come down and see that everything's all right. Now let's make some more space.' We pushed the table up against the wall. Then we fetched the twins out of the bedroom and put them on the rug so they could wriggle and wave their arms and legs in the air.

'I've cut some crusts off the bread, Lily. You can give them to the boys a bit later on. They like sucking on them.'

'I know what to do, Mum,' said Lily, who was thrilled to be in charge again.

'Don't let them get near the grate, will you?' said Mum as she put on her hat. Although the fire had gone out, the grate was still hot. Eddy and Frank were nine months old and they could roll about and get into trouble if you didn't watch them.

'I'll be careful, Mum,' said Lily, who obviously couldn't wait for us to leave.

'Good girl,' said Mum, kissing her on the forehead. 'But we won't be long.'

Not wanting to waste a minute, Mum quickly put on her hat and we hurried out of the house. The meeting was to be held in Bow Baths Hall and women were already walking in that direction. Some of them were in twos and threes, chatting to each other. I felt so thrilled to be going along – and very grown up. Would the suffragettes explain why women needed the vote, I wondered? And what would change if they got it? Maybe I'd find out this afternoon.

When we reached the hall, there was a lady standing in the doorway wearing a purple, green and white sash across her shoulder. She looked very important.

'I'm afraid all the seats are taken.' I really thought we weren't going to be let in. But then she said, 'You can stand at the back with me, if you like. I'm Mrs Stanbury. Pleased to meet you.' And she shook Mum's hand. 'Have you been to a meeting before?'

'No, I haven't,' said Mum. 'We read about it in one of the suffragettes' handbills.'

Mrs Stanbury smiled and started chatting. She was ever so friendly. 'We didn't have a suffrage group in Bow until Sylvia Pankhurst came to live here,' she said. 'It was her who started it up.'

I'd never heard of Sylvia Pankhurst but I thought she must be famous.

'Sylvia is the daughter of Emmeline Pankhurst,' Mrs Stanbury explained. 'She started the Women's Social and Political Union and Votes for Women and all that.'

A famous mother and a famous daughter. Fancy that! And I'd never heard of either of them. But things were getting very interesting.

Then Mrs Stanbury turned and looked anxiously towards the stage. 'We're hoping Miss Pankhurst will be well enough to speak to us this afternoon.'

'Has she been ill?' Mum asked.

'She's been in Holloway Prison,' Mrs Stanbury said in a low voice.

Well, I was shocked! The lady who was going to speak to us had been in prison. The shame of it! Only burglars and murderers went to prison, didn't they?

I waited for even more surprising information. And there was plenty to come.

'A few weeks ago, Miss Pankhurst was arrested on a march through London,' Mrs Stanbury told us. 'Lots of suffragettes were put in cells. The police said they were *disturbing the peace*, but they were doing no such thing.' She shook her head in disgust. 'Sylvia has been arrested so many times. It's terrible. Then she goes on hunger strike. Refuses to eat or drink.'

My mouth fell open in surprise. 'Why does she do that?' I asked. I couldn't imagine refusing food cos I never had enough. I was always hungry.

'She does it to protest!' said Mrs Stanbury. 'Then they force-feed her by pushing a tube right down her throat. It's torture! She nearly died this last time.'

Crikey! Could it get any worse? My stomach started to churn at the thought of it. Any minute, I was going to be sick.

'Is Miss Pankhurst all right now?' Mum asked.

'Well, they brought her back to Bow on a stretcher and . . .'

Luckily, before Mrs Stanbury could give us any more gruesome details, a lady in a long coat and a large grey hat stepped on to the stage and clapped her hands for silence. 'Good afternoon, everybody,' she said in a posh voice. 'I'm so pleased so many of you could come today. I think we'll be in for a very interesting meeting.' Then she looked at two or three women who were standing near us at the back of the hall. 'Would you close the doors please, ladies, and then we'll begin?'

Once they'd pushed the double doors closed, I heard the grating sound of metal as they slid four large bolts across so that the doors were shut fast. Now nobody would be able to get in. But why had they done that? Were they expecting trouble? It made me feel so nervous that I moved closer to Mum.

Eight

Once the doors were shut, the audience stopped their chatter and I was glad we were standing and not sitting on chairs. I could now see more easily over the tops of everybody's heads.

The lady in the grey hat spoke again. 'For our first speaker this afternoon,' she said, 'I'm delighted to introduce Miss Zelie Emerson, who we all know as a good friend of our society. She has been in prison many times for our cause. She also helped to set up our very own newspaper, the *Woman's Dreadnought*. So please give her a warm welcome. Zelie Emerson.'

Everybody clapped as the speaker marched on to the stage. Mrs Stanbury nudged Mum. 'She's a friend of Sylvia Pankhurst,' she whispered. 'An American.'

Zelie Emerson was quite a surprise. For one thing, she was small – not much taller than me. She wasn't wearing a hat and her black hair was cut short, like a boy's. Her clothing was quite ordinary – just a black skirt and a white blouse – but she had one of the biggest smiles I'd ever seen. As soon as I saw her, I knew I liked her. The trouble was when she spoke – oh dear!

'What's she saying, Mum?' I whispered. 'She's talking funny.'

'She's American,' Mum hissed.

I really struggled to understand what she was saying. I'd lived in Bow my whole life and I'd never heard anyone talk so strange. I'm sure I wasn't the only one in the room who felt like that – yet everybody else was nodding as she spoke as if they understood. They even clapped now and then. But to me, it was like a foreign language – so I stopped listening and started looking round the room.

It was then that I saw a man standing over by the stage. You couldn't miss him. He was very tall, dressed in black and looked as strong as an ox. Mrs Stanbury saw me staring.

'D'you know who that is?' she whispered.

I shook my head.

'That's Kosher Bill. He's a boxer and when there's trouble about, he often acts as Miss Pankhurst's bodyguard.'

'Is there going to be trouble?' I asked nervously – although, to be honest, I felt quite excited at the thought of it.

Mrs Stanbury shrugged. 'I don't know. But I think Miss Pankhurst must be in the building or why else would Kosher Bill be here, eh?'

Not long after that, Miss Emerson finished her talk, everybody clapped and she smiled before walking to the back of the stage. Then she held out her hand and helped a frail, white-faced woman walk to the front. As soon as the audience saw her, everyone got to their feet and the hall erupted with loud cheers.

'It's Miss Pankhurst,' said Mrs Stanbury. 'Oh, the poor thing. She can hardly walk. She doesn't look well, does she? How can the brutes have done this to her?'

Someone carried a chair on to the stage and Miss Pankhurst slowly sat down.

The room fell silent as everybody strained to hear what she had to say.

'Our movement is not only about votes for women,' she said, her voice thin and weak. 'It is about women's lives. We must get rid of the dreadful sweated labour. We must improve our children's welfare and education.'

There was a murmur of agreement around the room.

'To have a doctor to care for us when we are sick must be the right of all of us – not just the rich. And when we are old, we must have a pension to live on – not be sent to the workhouse to die. But how can we achieve all this?'

She paused and seemed to gasp for air. For a minute, I thought she was going to faint, but Zelie Emerson rushed on to the stage with a glass of water. We all waited, holding our breath to see if she would carry on.

Somehow, she found enough strength and began to speak again.

'For too long men have made the laws of this land.

But nothing improves. The lives of the poor are desperate and shameful.'

I heard mutters of agreement. The atmosphere in the hall was building. I could feel the excitement as Miss Pankhurst carried on.

'I ask you – are women not as intelligent and capable as men?'

Loud calls of 'Yes, yes, we are!' filled the room.

'Yet we are denied the education and careers of our brothers,' she said. 'Our lives are dictated by the needs and wishes of our husbands and fathers. Why should that be?'

As the hall exploded with shouts of agreement, I couldn't help thinking about Dad banning Mum from going to the meeting – and telling me I had to leave school. I guess Mum was thinking the same thing because she gave my hand a squeeze.

Looking exhausted, Miss Pankhurst's still went on: 'Women are not second-class citizens. Let women vote, I say, and watch the changes for good that we can make happen.'

Now finally I understood. These women weren't silly or crazy, they wanted to help, they wanted to change things, they wanted things to be fair. My heart soared as what she was saying sunk in.

But Miss Pankhurst didn't get to say any more. Suddenly there was banging on the doors and men shouting, 'Open up! Police!'

Everybody turned round, their eyes wide with fear. *Bang, bang, bang.* The police continued hammering on the door but nobody drew back the bolts. When the police realised they wouldn't be let inside, they began to ram the doors with something hard and solid until at last, the wood splintered and policemen burst in. As they ran right past us I was frozen with terror. Some women were clinging on to each other. Some were screaming as the police smashed chairs and swung their truncheons at anyone who blocked their way. It was a terrible sight. *Terrible.*

Luckily, by the time the policemen reached the stage, Miss Pankhurst had gone and so had Kosher Bill.

It all happened so quickly. I was rigid with fear and I couldn't move. Around me everyone was pushing and shoving and screaming. I looked for Mum and she grabbed me, pulling me close, fear in her eyes. Suddenly, Mrs Stanbury took hold of Mum's arm. 'Come with me, dearie,' she shouted. 'We need to get out of here as fast as we can.'

Women were already flooding out of the hall, desperately trying to get away. Some of them were carrying sticks to protect themselves from the police, and though it shocked me, I could understand why. Outside the hall, there were even more policemen, pushing and jostling. Kicking and thumping. Using their coshes whenever they felt like it. There were mounted police too, and you could get trampled under the horses' hooves if you weren't careful.

Right in front of me, a woman fell to the ground. But instead of helping her up, a policeman brought the sole of his boot down heavily on her back. Ignoring her screams, he swung his boot again, this time in to her ribs.

Women were yelling, 'Stop it! Stop it!' But it did no good.

'Keep moving, girl,' said Mrs Stanbury, pulling me away. 'We've got to go or we'll be pushed to the ground too.'

I was terrified. I saw two women being dragged away towards a police van – the Black Maria, people called it – and I knew they were being arrested.

Why were the police doing this? After all, it was just a meeting. The women weren't breaking the law. I didn't think they were, anyway.

'What can we do?' I said, wanting to stop and help. But Mum was pulling me along by one arm and Mrs Stanbury was tugging the other.

'I tell you – you've got to keep moving, girl,' said Mrs Stanbury, threading her way through the crowd. 'Come to my house. I only live round the corner.'

It was a great relief when we left the chaos behind and stood in front of Mrs Stanbury's front door.

'Now then,' she said stepping inside, 'what we need, my dears, is a nice cup of tea.'

Nine

Mr Stanbury was sitting in a chair by the fire, reading a newspaper. As we walked in, he put his paper on the table and stood up.

'How was it?' he asked his wife.

'Dreadful,' panted Mrs Stanbury, who was out of breath from running. 'Is there water in that kettle, Alfred? We're gasping for a drink.'

He nodded, lifted the kettle from the hearth and on to the fire.

'This is Mrs O'Doyle,' said Mrs Stanbury, 'and this is her daughter, Daisy.'

He shook Mum's hand and said, 'Here, have my chair. You look as white as a sheet.'

Mum barely whispered 'thank you' before she sank into his chair. Mrs Stanbury flopped into the other one and closed her eyes.

'Come and sit on the rug by the fire, young Daisy,' said Mr Stanbury. 'That kettle won't be long before it boils.'

Mr Stanbury was ever so kind. He let us rest while he made the tea himself and it was the best ever.

'So what happened?' he asked when we'd drained our cups.

'The police. That's what happened,' said Mrs Stanbury. 'Police brutality. They were after Miss Pankhurst, of course. Somehow they'd got wind that she was going to be at the meeting. They forced their way in and set upon the women in a way I would never have believed possible.'

Mr Stanbury packed tobacco into his pipe and lit it. 'Well, we've had detectives hanging around Bow for weeks now. They've known Jessie Payne's been looking after Miss Pankhurst since she came out of Holloway Prison.' He drew on his pipe. 'They've obviously just been waiting till she left the Paynes' house so they could arrest her again.'

Mrs Stanbury smiled. 'Well, they didn't get her, Alfred. I think Kosher Bill must have carried her out the back of the hall somehow.'

Although colour had returned to Mum's cheeks, I could tell she was feeling anxious.

'Thank you for the tea but we need to be getting off,' she said. 'Do you think the police will have gone by now?'

Mr Stanbury, seeing how worried she was, patted her on the shoulder. 'You stay there, lass. I'll walk round the corner and see what's going on.'

He was back in five minutes. 'They've gone,' he said. 'You'll be safe enough to walk home now. There's just a few women gossiping at the end of the road.'

Mum smiled and got out of the chair. 'Thank you

both for your help. I don't know what we'd have done without you.'

Mrs Stanbury held Mum's hand. 'It's a pity we didn't hear more from Miss Pankhurst.'

'Oh, it was grand,' said Mum. 'She talked so much sense.'

'She was amazing,' I agreed.

Mr Stanbury stood up and handed his newspaper to Mum. 'Here, take this, lass. You'll find it interesting reading.'

I saw it was the *Woman's Dreadnought*.

'Is that the suffragettes' paper they talked about at the meeting?' I asked.

'It is,' said Mr Stanbury. 'In fact, we're looking for young ladies to deliver 'em round here. Are you interested?'

I nodded my head vigorously and glanced at Mum.

'Think about it, Daisy,' said Mrs Stanbury. 'I work at Arber's printing works on Roman Road. You can always pop in and see me if you decide to help. Now off you go. You two have had enough excitement for one day.'

We hurried home and, as we turned into Tuttle Street, we spotted Dad outside our front door, smoking his pipe. When he saw us, his face turned black as thunder.

'Get inside, both of you,' he said. 'Stop them babies crying. And when you've done that, you can tell me where you've been all this time.'

Eddy and Frank were screaming their little heads off. Lily had taken them into the bedroom. She was sitting with them on the bed, tears streaming down her face.

'They won't stop crying,' she sobbed.

Mum picked up Eddy and I picked up Frank.

'Don't you worry, Lily,' said Mum, kissing her forehead. 'They just want something to eat, that's all. I'm sorry we're so late back. It's not your fault.'

With bread and milk inside them, the twins soon quietened down. Dad came in and sat in his chair, sulking.

'Well, I must say, that was quite a noise,' said Mum, trying to be cheerful. 'But they should sleep for a while now, Patrick. You'll have some peace and quiet.'

'A man should expect peace and quiet on a Sunday,' Dad grumbled. 'When I got back from Tom's I expected my wife to be at home looking after my children.'

'I thought you and Tom were going to the Gunmaker's,' said Mum.

'Well, we didn't,' Dad replied. 'But what's that got to do with it? Where've you been all this time?'

I held my breath, wondering what Mum was going to say. Would she make up a lie or would she tell the truth?

'We went to a meeting at the Bow Baths Hall, that's all,' she said.

'Bow Baths Hall? A meeting?' Dad paused for a second, thinking. 'You mean that suffragette meeting? The one on that handbill that Daisy read out?'

'Yes.'

His face flushed red. 'I said you weren't to go!' he

said, slapping his hand on the table. 'I said you were to stay at home, didn't I?'

Suddenly there was a flash of anger in Mum's eyes. 'Am I your slave, Patrick O'Doyle? Must I do your bidding every minute of the day?'

'If I say so, then you must!' he said. 'I'll not have you mixing with them suffragettes. Before you know it, I'll be the laughing stock of the factory. Have you thought about that?'

Mum tried to stay calm. 'The suffragettes want to make things better for women, that's all, Patrick.'

'Do they?' Dad growled. 'And who's going to make things better for *me*?'

And with that, he stormed out of the house.

Ten

'Now, girls,' said Mum. 'You know your father doesn't mean half of what he says. He'll have a walk about and he'll come home as right as rain and it'll all be forgotten.'

I wasn't sure Mum believed that. I certainly didn't. I think she was saying it to make Lily and me feel better.

Then I remembered the newspaper. It was folded up in my pocket.

'Shall I get rid of this before Dad gets back?'

'Maybe – but why don't you read me a bit from it first,' said Mum, fetching her sewing box. 'Let's see what's going on.'

I unfolded the paper and spread it on the table while Mum began darning a large hole in Dad's sock.

'There's a piece here by Emmeline Pankhurst,' I said.

'Who's she?' asked Lily.

'She's a famous suffragette,' Mum replied. 'She's the mother of Sylvia Pankhurst – the lady we saw at the meeting this afternoon.'

Lily looked puzzled. I don't think she understood.

I traced my finger over the words in the newspaper and read out loud. 'Mrs Pankhurst says that women must keep up the fight for the vote – breaking windows, blowing up pillar boxes, slashing paintings. Whatever it takes.'

'Oh dear,' said Mum. 'I don't like that at all. No wonder they get put in prison. I really don't approve of violence.'

I read some more. 'She says that after fifty years of peaceful protests by Mrs Fawcett's suffragists, women still haven't got the vote. So now suffragettes must make themselves such a nuisance that the government will have to take notice.'

Mum shook her head. 'I can't agree with her. Life's hard enough without all that trouble, Daisy.'

I read on. 'Mrs Pankhurst says that the laws of this land were made by men. If women must live by these laws, women should have a say in making them too.'

I looked up at Mum. 'Well, that makes sense,' she said. 'If we don't have the vote, we can't have any say in making laws, can we? So I think Mrs Pankhurst is right about that.'

'Stop talking about Mrs Pank,' said Lily, climbing on Mum's knee. 'I want a story! Go on, Mum. Tell us *Red Riding Hood*.'

Poor Lily! She was too young to understand grown-up things. I folded up the paper and put it in my pocket. I could read the rest later.

Mum finished her darning and dropped Dad's sock on the table. Lily curled up, sucking her thumb, listening to fairy tales. And when her head began to nod, Mum told a story for me – the one about Florence Nightingale. How she rebelled against her parents. How she went to the war in Crimea. How she set up amazing hospitals and how she helped injured and sick soldiers. I knew the story by heart. And it was every bit as exciting as the first time I heard it.

That night, I lay in bed thinking about what I'd read in the paper and what I'd heard Sylvia Pankhurst say that afternoon. If everybody did a bit to help, I thought, things might get done to make our lives better. And maybe one day, I'd go to that school for nursing. That should be possible, shouldn't it?

So this is what I decided: I wouldn't go smashing windows or chaining myself to Buckingham Palace's railings. The violence I'd seen at the meeting was terrifying. But I could do something small to start with. Mr Stanbury had asked if I'd deliver the *Woman's Dreadnought* newspaper. I could do that surely. After school tomorrow, I'd go to Arber's printing works and tell Mrs Stanbury I'd do it. Mum and Dad needn't know. I thought Mum would be pleased, but I didn't want to cause another row. I'd do it on my own and I'd be a secret suffragette.

Eleven

After school on Monday, Mrs Rosen agreed to keep an eye on Lily and the twins again while I went over to Arber's printing works, which wasn't far away on Roman Road. I'd walked past it lots of times but I'd never been inside or taken much notice of it. There was a large shop window crammed with handbills and adverts and books. Over the top were the words 'Arber and Co. Ltd'. There was a door next to the window and, as I pushed it open, a bell tinkled. Behind the counter, leaning over some kind of printing machine, was Mrs Stanbury.

'Why, Daisy,' she said, wiping her ink-covered hands on her apron. 'How very nice to see you! What can I do for you, my dear?'

I took a deep breath. 'You asked me if I'd like to deliver the *Woman's Dreadnought*,' I said nervously.

Her face lit up. 'And would you?' she said. I just stood there nodding. 'Oh, that's wonderful. People have paid to have them delivered, you see. But we're short of people to do it. It's the houses over by Victoria Park and even further away. It could take you an hour or more. Can you manage that?'

My stomach sank. I daren't be away for that long.

I needed to be home before Mum and Dad got back from work. If Dad found out I was helping the suffragettes, he'd be furious, and he'd blame Mum for taking me to that meeting. But this was my first chance to help. If I failed, what would Mrs Stanbury think? What would Sylvia Pankhurst think? She'd been to prison for what she believed in. She'd been on hunger strike! Now here was I, worried about delivering a few newspapers.

Mrs Stanbury must have seen the worry on my face. 'Of course,' she said, 'you don't have to deliver them all at once. You could take half today and the rest tomorrow. Would that be better?' And she smiled.

'It would,' I said, relieved that she had solved my problem. 'As long as I'm home before Mum and Dad.'

So that was settled. She took me into the back room where there were two printing machines – very smelly and very noisy.

'These are the newspapers,' Mrs Stanbury said, pointing to several piles on a shelf. She lifted one pile down and carried it through to the shop.

'I'll write the address on top of each newspaper,' she said, putting them on the counter and picking up a pencil. 'So you'll know where to go.'

Once she'd marked all the papers, she put them into a large bag with 'Votes for Women' printed on the side.

'I like the bag,' I said as I slipped the strap over my shoulder. 'I feel like a real suffragette.'

Mrs Stanbury laughed. 'Those stripes on the strap

are our colours – purple, white and green. Purple for loyalty, white for purity and green for hope.'

'They're lovely,' I said. 'Really nice.'

I was ready to go, excited to be working for the suffragettes.

'Thank you for coming,' Mrs Stanbury said as she opened the door for me. 'When you've finished the delivery, there'll be tuppence waiting for you, Daisy. It's yours, for helping out.'

'Thank you, Mrs Stanbury,' I said, amazed that I was being paid. 'And I'll come again tomorrow.'

I set off towards Victoria Park to deliver the first batch of the *Dreadnought*. The houses were big there and some had steps leading up to the front door. Almost half of the houses had ordered newspapers. I didn't realise so many people supported the suffragettes.

I'd been gone for half an hour or so and had turned up a side street to deliver the last lot, when somebody shouted, 'Oi! You! What you doin' up here?'

I spun round and saw a grubby man about as old as Dad, leaning against a wall with a pipe in his hand.

At first, I wasn't going to speak. I was just going to walk away. But then I said to myself, 'Be brave, Daisy. Stand up to him. Remember you're working for the suffragettes now.'

'I'm delivering the *Woman's Dreadnought*,' I said boldly, even though really I was shaking in my boots.

The man didn't say anything. Instead he started

walking towards me and I desperately wanted to run away. But I was so terrified, I couldn't move.

When he was up close he said, 'Delivering the *Dreadnought*, are yer?' Then he smirked. 'Don't say them mad women have been filling your head with that suffragette tosh? Huh! Then you can expect to get stuffed in gaol like all the others. And quite right too.'

I opened my mouth to speak but no sound came out – just a croak. The man leaned forward and clamped his hand on my shoulder. He was so close to me that I could smell his beery breath and I felt sick.

Then someone shouted, 'Arthur Gittings!'

It was a woman from the top of the street.

'Arthur Gittings!' she shouted again. 'Leave that girl alone or I'll go straight round to your wife and tell her what you're up to.'

The man dropped his hand and stepped away.

'I'm not up to nothin',' he replied.

'Then get off back to the ale house where you belong,' she yelled as she marched down the street, flapping her hand, ready to give him a taste of his own medicine.

He turned and scuttled away round the corner and out of her reach. I shouldn't have been frightened of him. He was a real worm!

When the woman reached me, she smiled and said, 'Are you all right, dearie?'

I nodded.

'I expect you've got my *Dreadnought*, have you?'

I glanced down at the paper in my hand. 'Number twenty-two?'

'That's right,' she said, and took it from me. 'I like to keep up with everything.' Then she put her hand on my shoulder. 'Now don't you take no notice of men like Arthur Gittings. Women round here won't put up with the likes of him. Not since Miss Pankhurst came to Bow and taught us to stand up for ourselves.'

There was that name again! Until yesterday, I'd never heard of her.

Then she told me Miss Pankhurst had been organising self-defence lessons for women. 'You can come along if you like, dearie. You never know when it'll come in handy.'

I pulled myself up to my full height. 'Thank you,' I said. 'That sounds like a good idea.' I didn't think Dad would let me go but maybe when things got better, I'd join in.

I set off to deliver the rest of the papers, already feeling more like one of the suffragettes.

Twelve

Roman Road market was a great place to visit. You didn't need any money to go along and look at the stalls. Lily and me often took the babies down there on a Saturday, because Mum and Dad had to work even though there was no school. But our brothers, they were getting bigger.

'Eddy's really heavy now, Daisy,' said Lily. 'I can't carry him all the way to the market.'

'I've got an idea,' I said.

I found an old blanket, folded it over Lily's shoulder and tied it round her middle. Then I tucked Eddy inside so that the blanket held him like a sling.

'How's that?'

Lily smiled. 'That's good, Daisy. He doesn't feel heavy now.'

So we set off and by the time we reached the market, the street was busy with people out in the sunshine looking to buy a treat. There were stalls full of fruit and vegetables and I was tempted to reach into my pocket and spend the four pennies I'd earned from Mrs Stanbury in the week. But I didn't. Lily would be sure to say something and Dad would be furious when he learned how I'd earned them.

We passed one stall selling second-hand clothes.

'Look at that, Daisy,' said Lily, pointing to a pretty dress covered in blue flowers hanging high up on the stall. 'It's beautiful! Will you ask Mum to buy it for me? Will you, Daisy?'

I shook my head. 'I don't think it would fit you, Lily.'

'It will, Daisy. It will,' she said, bouncing up and down. 'Can we ask if I can try it on?'

I glanced at the lady standing behind the stall and I pulled a face. She knew straight away that I didn't have the money to buy the blue dress.

She leaned towards Lily and said, 'Sorry, dearie. That dress is too small for a big girl like you.'

Lily stuck out her lip in disappointment. I took hold of her hand and we walked on.

The next stall was selling antiques. There were all kinds of things – old chairs, brass candlesticks and beautiful old lamps. But they were expensive and there was nothing we could ever hope to have in our house.

As we turned to move on, I saw something that made me stop in my tracks. Right there, next to the antique stall, was a table covered in a white cloth with the words 'Votes for Women' embroidered on it. Standing in front of the stall was a lady giving out handbills to passers-by. The suffragettes had set up a stall of their own.

'Well I never!' said the lady with the handbills. 'If it isn't Daisy!'

I blinked and stared. There stood Mrs Stanbury, smiling her lovely wide smile.

'Hello, Mrs Stanbury,' I said. 'We've just come for a walk.'

'And is this your little sister?'

I nodded and Lily said, 'I'm six and I'm called Lily and this is my brother, Eddy.' She pulled the blanket back a little and Eddy peeped up at Mrs Stanbury with his big blue eyes. 'He's only a baby. He's not even one yet.'

'My word!' said Mrs Stanbury, laughing. 'He's a fine young man, I must say.' Then she turned to me. 'And who's this little bundle, Daisy?' she asked.

'This is Eddy's twin,' I said. 'He's called Frank.'

The twins never liked meeting new people and they suddenly set up a terrible wailing until they were quite red in the face. Mrs Stanbury, kind as ever, beckoned us to go round the back of the stall where two ladies were sitting on a bench. When they saw the babies, they reached out and took them from us and made such a fuss of them that the twins soon stopped crying.

'We love babies, don't we, Ethel?' said a small lady called Mrs Savoy. They were both so friendly that Lily stayed with them and chatted while Mrs Stanbury took me to see the things the suffragettes had spread out on the table.

'I've never seen a suffragettes' stall,' I said.

'We've got all kinds of things, Daisy. Look, there's a

62

pile of the *Woman's Dreadnought*. We sell quite a lot from the stall.'

But as well as the newspapers, there were handbills advertising meetings and some lovely rosettes in purple, green and white with 'Votes for Women' printed in the middle.

'Would you like one?' Mrs Stanbury asked. 'You worked so hard delivering the newspapers, I think you deserve it.'

'Oh, thank you, I'd love one, Mrs Stanbury. But I'm still not sure I even know what "Votes for Women" means.' I was a bit embarrassed to ask, but if I was going to be a secret suffragette I needed to know. 'My dad says it's all just nonsense.'

'Lots of people feel like that about politics, Daisy,' Mrs Stanbury said kindly. 'But things won't change unless more people get the vote. If women get to choose the politicians, then the politicians will have to make laws that help us, see?'

I nodded – it was so simple, but it finally made sense.

I felt so proud when she pinned the rosette on my dress, and I was sure that one day I'd be able to vote to help make things better.

'If you like, Mrs Stanbury, I'll give out the handbills,' I said. 'You could go and sit down for a bit.'

She smiled and nodded. 'Thank you, Daisy. I could do with a rest.' And she went to join the others.

I read the handbill, which was about a meeting in

a week's time. Members of Parliament were speaking at the Civic Hall and the suffragettes planned to hold a protest outside. That sounded exciting. If I could persuade Mum to go then I'd go with her. After all, I was now a secret suffragette and I wanted to join in the protest. Isn't that what Miss Pankhurst asked us to do? I didn't want to get put in prison or anything, but I could shout 'Votes for Women' outside the Civic Hall. And if things got scary like they did at Bow Baths, at least I'd be ready this time.

My stomach was suddenly filled with bubbles of excitement as I realised that I was part of a huge campaign. Me! Daisy O'Doyle! I couldn't believe it! I was so excited that, instead of just standing by the stall, I started to jump about waving a handbill over my head and shouting, 'Votes for Women! Votes for Women! Come to the protest meeting next week.'

I must have looked crazy, bouncing around like a jack-in-the-box. But I kept on shouting. Most people stared at me. Some of them laughed, but I didn't mind because some took a handbill. In fact, I gave away so many that I had to fetch more off the table. I was really proud of myself.

I'd been doing that for quite a while when, to my surprise, I saw a familiar face. Mrs Pidgeon was heading in my direction, struggling through the market, leaning heavily on a walking stick. It was a long way for her to walk because she had terrible trouble with her knees.

When she spotted me, she smiled and waved and I ran over to her.

'My goodness, Daisy,' she said, 'I didn't know you were a suffragette.'

'I'd really like to be one but I'm just helping today,' I said. 'It's a secret. You won't tell Mum, will you?'

Mrs Pidgeon smiled. 'Not if you don't want me to, dearie.'

I passed her a handbill. 'Will you be going to the protest meeting next week, Mrs Pidgeon?' I asked.

But she shook her head. 'I'm afraid I'm not up to that kind of thing, Daisy. I've heard that the police can be quite violent.'

I shrugged, not knowing what to say.

'But I do agree that women should have the vote,' she said.

'Do you really?' I asked, surprised that an old lady like Mrs Pidgeon would be interested in the suffragettes.

'Well, look at me, dearie. I've worked all my life standing in a factory from morning till night, six days a week. Now my poor legs have given way, I'm left with nothing to look forward to but the workhouse.' She shook her head as if she was imagining that terrible future. 'If women had their say, things would be different. We'd make the law so everybody would be looked after. I know we would.'

She put her hand on my shoulder and patted it. 'You help 'em get the vote, my girl. Keep at it. You mustn't give up.'

Thirteen

I was really proud of the rosette Mrs Stanbury had given me, but as soon as I got home, I hid it under the bed where Dad wouldn't see it.

Lily, as always, was bursting with news and couldn't wait to tell Mum and Dad what she'd been up to. I was worried that she'd tell them about the suffragettes' stall and what I'd done. But I needn't have worried. When Mum and Dad arrived home from the factory, Lily just went on and on about the blue dress she'd seen.

'It was so pretty,' she said. 'It had flowers on it and I really want it, Mum. I think it would fit me just right. Can I have it? Can I? Please?'

Mum smiled as she took off her hat and hung it on the peg. 'I don't think so, poppet,' she said.

Lily didn't give up. 'But I've had this dress for ever such a long time,' she whined, 'and it used to be Daisy's and I want a dress of my own. Please, Mum! Pleeeeease!'

Mum couldn't help laughing but she still shook her head. 'They cost a lot of money, my love.'

Dad was sitting in his chair stuffing tobacco into his pipe. 'We can't afford to buy dresses, Lily,' he said. 'Your mother will make you one when the time is right.

We've no money these days. Just remember that. There's nothing wrong with the dress you've got.' And nothing more was said about it.

That Saturday night, we went to bed early because Mum was going to wash our clothes. She'd borrowed a tub from Mrs Rosen upstairs and filled it with two buckets of water. She intended to scrub away at our clothes while we were in bed and hang them to dry on the clothes horse in front of the fire. But that night, we had no coal. There was no money to buy any – what with Mrs Griggs demanding an extra penny – so when we woke up the next morning, our clothes were still wet.

I groaned and Lily snivelled very loudly because we'd have to stay in till they dried.

'If you hang 'em out on Mrs Rosen's line, they'll dry in no time,' I said. 'It's a fine day, Mum, and the wind's blowing.'

Mum raised her eyebrows in surprise. 'It's Sunday, Daisy. I can't hang washing across the street today, can I? What would the neighbours think?'

So the clothes had to stay on the clothes horse and that meant it could be tomorrow before they were dry.

'No complaining now,' said Mum. 'Just think how nice you'll look when you go to school tomorrow in clean clothes.'

Then Mum went to fetch water from the standpipe. I knew what that meant.

'Now wash your hands and faces,' she said, handing

us the flannel. 'And don't forget the back of your neck and behind your ears.' She was very particular about them. I don't know why.

Once we were washed and dried, we wrapped ourselves in a blanket and sat on the rug, playing with Eddy and Frank. Mum was patching Dad's shirt while he hammered a bit of leather over a hole in his boot. He was going to take Great-Aunt Maude to Mass, as he always did on Sunday morning. Lily and I didn't like Great-Aunt Maude much. She was always saying things like 'Silence is golden' and 'Little girls should be seen and not heard'. Which we found very difficult – if not impossible.

For the rest of Sunday morning, I sat there staring at the dresses hanging on the clothes horse, willing them to dry. That afternoon, I was hoping to meet with Eliza in the park. We'd got so much to talk about. I'd been thinking about her all week, hoping she was happier at the jam factory now. Maybe they'd paid her a bit more this week. I hoped so. But I was desperate to tell her about the suffragettes and how they were fighting for fair wages. I knew it would cheer her up to know that things might change soon.

But it didn't happen. The clothes didn't dry soon enough and that meant we couldn't go out and I couldn't meet Eliza in the park. It turned out to be a really miserable day.

Fourteen

The next morning, our clothes were finally dry and we looked very smart as we walked to school.

Now that I was a secret suffragette, I promised myself to behave perfectly in class. I would work hard. I would not be boastful. I would not be rude to Miss Spike, no matter how difficult that was.

I think she was surprised by my change of behaviour because, at the end of the day, she said, 'Daisy O'Doyle, you're a clever girl when you put your mind to it.'

I already knew I was clever but it was good to hear her say it.

'Thank you, Miss Spike,' I said, as polite as anybody in the whole of Bow.

But after that, nothing good happened. It was another awful day.

When Lily and I got back with the twins, we were surprised to find that Mum was already at home. She was sitting bent over the table, her head in her hands. It was obvious to me that something was wrong.

Lily didn't realise that, though. She ran inside squealing, 'Mum! Mum!' She was so pleased to see her.

When Mum looked up, I was shocked to see that her

eyes were red and swollen and her cheeks were wet with tears.

I put Frank down on the rug and wrapped my arms round Mum's shoulders. 'What is it?' I said. 'What's happened? Has Dad been hurt?'

She shook her head as she wiped her tears on her sleeve. 'No. No,' she said and she tried to smile.

'Then what's happened? What's wrong?'

It was some time before she managed to get the words out. 'They . . . They . . . They sacked me,' she said. 'I've lost my job. What are we going to do?' Then she broke down in tears again.

I didn't understand. 'Why did they do that?' I asked. 'You've worked there a long time and you're a good worker. Everyone says so.'

She nodded and tried to calm down. 'It's just not right, Daisy,' she said. 'The factory owner saw a woman eating bread in the middle of the afternoon. So he sacked her. She was almost fainting from hunger, poor woman. She hadn't had a proper break since seven this morning.'

'But why did they sack you too?'

'Because I stood up for her,' she said, holding her hands up in despair. 'There are sixteen of us women in the top room. We're crammed in like peas in a pod working on the sewing machines. Then there's the heat from the coals for the pressing irons. It's like an inferno. There's no air and we can hardly breathe. I've known women faint in there.' Mum wiped tears from her cheek.

70

'Did you know, the men in the factory are allowed a break? They have somewhere to eat a sandwich. But not us women.'

I could see Mum was angry now.

'We have no break and nowhere to go. Some of us sneak into the privies to eat. Isn't that disgusting? And that's what I told the factory owner as he stood there in his fine suit and his silk cravat.'

'You told the factory owner? Oh, Mum, what did he say?'

'He said I was a troublemaker. That I probably wanted to join a union.'

'But that's not true,' I protested. 'You're not a troublemaker.'

'No, it isn't true. But I wish I *was* in a union,' she said. 'The women at Bryant and May got a union.'

'I don't remember that, Mum.'

'It was a long time ago, Daisy,' she said. 'They went on strike and stood up for themselves. They formed the Matchmakers' Trade Union and they've got decent working conditions now. Maybe that's what everybody should do. Stand up to the bosses.' I couldn't help thinking of Miss Pankhurst and her fine words.

'But you didn't say that to the factory owner, did you, Mum?'

'No, I didn't,' she said, wiping her hand across her eyes. 'It was really Fred Pollock that did for me. He told the owner there'd been talk in the factory.'

71

'What do you mean "talk"?' I asked Mum.

'I was seen at the suffragette meeting last Sunday when the police were called.'

'But you didn't do anything wrong, Mum.'

'I know. But as far as the owner was concerned, I must have been breaking the law if I was there. He was furious and said he wasn't having any suffragettes in his factory.'

I put my arm round Mum's shoulders as she broke down in tears.

'How will we do without my wage, Daisy?' she sobbed. 'We can't manage as it is. And what's your father going to say when he comes home?'

It was all too much. She laid her head on the table, still crying.

'You'll get another job, Mum. I'll go round to Mrs Stanbury and see what she's got to say. I bet she'll be able to help. Those women want to help people like us.' I turned to Lily. 'You look after Mum and the boys. I'm going out.'

Mum held out her hand and tried to stop me but I was too quick and I ran out of the door.

Fifteen

Mrs Stanbury wasn't surprised to see me when I walked through the door of Arber's printing works. It was my day for delivering the *Dreadnought*, after all.

'Ready and waiting for you, Daisy,' she called as she reached over for the bag.

But I just stood there – a bit embarrassed – hardly knowing what to say. Mrs Stanbury could tell there was something wrong. She stepped out from behind the counter and took hold of my hands. 'Whatever is it, lass?' she said. 'What's the matter?'

'It's . . . it's my mum,' I stammered.

'Is she sick?'

'She's been sacked for helping a woman at the factory . . . and for being at a suffragette meeting.' By then I was sobbing. '. . . and it's not fair cos she's worked there for ages . . . and she's a good worker . . . and now she hasn't got a job and Dad will go mad.' I gabbled on and on as tears poured down my face. 'She was only sticking up for another woman who was in trouble. It wasn't her fault.'

Mrs Stanbury fetched a stool. 'Sit down here, Daisy,

and wipe your eyes,' she said, giving me a large cotton handkerchief. 'Now slow down and tell me all about it.'

So I told her everything and when I'd finished, she said, 'Now listen to me, Daisy. That's a terrible thing to have happened. And you're quite right – it isn't fair. There are too many things in this life that aren't fair. That's why we women must stick together and fight to change 'em.'

She smiled and pulled up another stool and sat next to me. I could tell that she understood how desperate it was for our family.

'The papers can wait,' she said. 'You go home and look after your mother. I expect she's feeling awful.' Then she looked me right in the eye as if she could see into my head. 'And listen, Daisy. You're to tell her that there's a job at Arber's, if she wants it. We could do with another hand in the print shop. Young Annie's been taken ill and we're so busy with the *Dreadnought* and suffragette posters and handbills, we can hardly keep up.'

She waited for me to say something. But I couldn't speak.

'It's all right, Daisy,' she said. 'I'm in charge here. I can take people on when it's needed. So how about it? Do you think your mum would like working here?'

I couldn't believe what I was hearing. There was a job for Mum!

'Well now,' she said, knowing that I'd been struck

dumb. 'You must get off home. Go on, Daisy, and give your mum the news!'

I was bursting with gratitude. I'd come to Mrs Stanbury hoping she would be able to help. But I hadn't expected her to solve Mum's problems so quickly.

'Thank you, Mrs Stanbury,' I said when I'd recovered my voice. 'Thanks ever so much. I can't wait to tell her.'

I ran so fast that, by the time I got home, I was out of breath. 'You'll never guess what, Mum!' I gasped as I burst through the door.

Mum was sitting with Frank on her knee and Lily was in Dad's chair bouncing Eddy up and down.

'Where've you been, Daisy?' said Mum. 'You just went running off like a wild thing. I was worried.'

'I told you. I went to see Mrs Stanbury. You remember, the lady we met at Bow Baths Hall.'

'Yes, I remember. She was very kind.'

'I know . . . She works at Arber's printing works and . . .' I took a deep breath before telling her the amazing news. 'Well . . . she says you can go and work there. They need somebody. You can start tomorrow, if you want!'

I thought she'd be pleased. I expected her face to light up at the news, but instead it clouded over. Didn't she understand what I'd just told her?

I tried again. 'Mrs Stanbury says Arber's is ever so busy. Did you know they do the printing for the suffragettes – handbills, posters, newspapers – the lot?'

'Yes, I know that, Daisy,' Mum said, turning away. 'It's very kind of Mrs Stanbury and I'm proud of you for trying to help. But I can't work there. Your father wouldn't put up with that. You know what he thinks of the suffragettes.'

'But Mum . . .'

'No, Daisy. He's going to be upset enough about me losing my job. I can't do it. I can't work at Arber's.'

Sixteen

Sometime later, Dad came storming through the front door. 'What do you think you're playing at?' he yelled at Mum. I'd never seen him so angry and he'd never *ever* shouted like that at her.

Lily and I had one thought – to get out of the way and hide in the bedroom. But Dad grabbed hold of us before we could get there. 'Stay where you are. You two had better hear this as well.'

We didn't dare move. Lily looked terrified. Her lips were quivering and her eyes were the size of marbles. I wanted to put my arms round her, but I daren't. As for Mum, she must have been scared too. She didn't even look at Dad. She sat with her eyes cast down and her shoulders slumped.

Dad sank into his chair and turned to us. 'Do you know what your mother did today?' he said. 'Eh? Do yer?'

We stood there shaking our heads because we were too scared to do anything else.

'Well, I'll tell you. She was rude to the owner of the factory. *Rude!* Telling him how to run the place. Can you imagine that, eh?'

We shook our heads again.

'It was all round the factory this afternoon. My wife's a *suffragette*. That's what they're sayin'. And all because your mother thinks she's got *rights*.'

When he said the word 'rights' he thumped his fist on the table.

'But she ain't got rights. She's my *wife*, that's what she is. If she thinks she can speak her mind whenever she feels like it, then she's *wrong*. And that's why she lost her job. Do you understand?'

Too frightened to speak, we nodded.

Then Dad turned to look at Mum. 'So . . . what have you got to say for yourself?'

Mum's voice came out in a whisper. 'I was just trying to help Nellie.'

'HELP?' yelled Dad. 'Why were you helping somebody else? It wasn't any of your business, was it?'

Mum flinched but then she took a deep breath and leaned forward across the table. She didn't rage. She didn't shout. She kept her voice steady.

'A woman had been sacked for eating a piece of bread. I had to say something. She's got three kids to look after and she's practically starving. How could I stand by and say nothing?'

'Never mind *her*,' said Dad, thumping the table again. 'Thanks to you, it won't be long before our own kids are starving.'

Suddenly, Mum snapped as if she could stand it

no longer. 'And what would you have done, Patrick O'Doyle?' she asked, her face filled with anger. 'Nothing. That's what most men would do, isn't it? Nothing!'

Without warning, Dad stood and raised his hand as though he was going to slap Mum across her cheek. Lily screamed.

'No, Dad!' I shouted. 'No!'

He stopped just in time and looked down at his hand as though he didn't recognise it as his own.

'Well, it seems you're just like your father after all, Patrick,' said my mother quietly.

'What do you expect, woman?' said Dad. 'You've made me a laughing stock in the factory,' he growled. 'They're sayin' I can't control my own wife. Did you know that? How do you think that makes me feel, eh?' He wiped spittle from his mouth with the back of his hand.

'Why should a wife be controlled, anyway?' said Mum.

'There you go again with your silly suffragette talk and ideas about your rights. Well, from now on, I'll make sure I control you, lady! You can work at home and look after the babies. And no more mixing with them suffragette la-di-das.'

Mum was still sitting in her chair, and I could see she was shaking – from fear and anger, I think.

'In all the years we've been together, Patrick O'Doyle, you've never raised your hand to me,' she sobbed.

I was desperate to put my arms round her but Dad sent us to bed.

In one way it was a relief. Now I didn't have to see his angry face. We climbed on to the bed and curled up together. Lily cried quietly into my chest while I lay there worrying about Mum and Dad. There had never been such anger in our family. Things had never been violent between them before, but I couldn't help wondering if our problems were going to get even worse.

Seventeen

The next morning, nobody spoke much. Dad was quieter than usual. I think he must have felt bad for losing his temper like that.

We went to school as usual. Lily ran over to her friends and I walked across the schoolyard to where the older girls gathered. I noticed that lots of them were giving me funny looks. Nobody waved or said 'hello'. In fact, some even turned their backs on me.

Then Minnie Unwin came hurrying towards me with a nasty smirk on her face. 'It's all over Bow,' she said.

'What is?'

'Your mum's been sacked, ain't she?' she said, placing her hands on her hips. 'She's one of them crazy suffragettes.'

I ignored her and walked past.

'My mum says she ought to be ashamed of herself,' she shouted after me. 'Mixing with them toffee-nosed troublemakers. No wonder they wouldn't have her at the factory.'

I stopped and spun round to face her. 'For your information, my mum was sacked cos she stood up for another woman who'd lost her job,' I said. 'I don't suppose you'd dare to stand up for anybody, Minnie Unwin. You're as weak as a yard of pump water. Now leave me alone or I'll show you me fist.'

Nobody spoke to me for the rest of that day. I kept my head down and worked hard and was relieved when the bell was rung for the end of school.

Lily was waiting for me in the yard. 'I'm glad Mum's at home, aren't you, Daisy?' she asked as we walked out of the school gates.

'Yes,' I replied, although I didn't really mean it.

'She's looking after the babies now, so we won't have to fetch them from Mrs Griggs, will we?' Lily chatted on. 'I don't like Mrs Griggs, do you?'

'Not much,' I said. But as I spoke, something crossed my mind. Now Mum wasn't working at the factory, it was going to be difficult for me to slip out and deliver the *Dreadnought*. I didn't want to give that up. After all, I'd promised to help and I couldn't break that promise. Not when they'd given me a suffragette rosette. But being seen with the suffragettes had caused enough trouble already in my family. So what could I do?

When we arrived home, the twins were on the rug and Mum was busy at the table. She had rolled up the sleeves of her blouse and was stuffing straw into bits of material.

'What are you doing?' asked Lily.

Mum pushed a lock of hair back off her forehead. 'I'm stuffing toys,' she said.

Lily was thrilled. 'Toys for us?' she asked.

'No, darlin',' said Mum, kissing Lily's cheek. 'Dad went to see a man called Mr Fredericks last night. He came round this morning and he's agreed to pay me for stuffing toys.'

'That's good news,' I said.

Lily went to play with the babies and Mum looked up at me, her eyes filled with bitterness. 'It feels like slave labour, Daisy,' she said in a low voice so that Lily wouldn't hear.

I could tell she was angry. No wonder! She'd been treated badly by the factory boss and by Dad. She looked down at the toy rabbit she was stuffing and pushed it away.

'From now on, I'll be working all hours just to earn a few shillings. Heaven help me,' she said, wiping her cheeks with the back of her hand. 'If you ask me, the suffragettes are the only people talking sense round here.'

This might be the time to let Mum into my secret, I thought. I felt really nervous but I took a deep breath and said, 'I've got something to tell you, Mum.'

'What is it, Daisy?' she asked and smiled.

The only way I could do it was to gabble it all out in one go. *Very fast.*

'I promised to deliver the *Dreadnought* on the other side of Bow, this afternoon. I did it last week too. Mrs Stanbury gives me tuppence every time. But I'd do it for nothing, really. The suffragettes want to make things better, don't they? They want us to be able to vote for things that are important. That's what we want too, ain't it, Mum?' By the time I'd finished, I was out of breath.

Mum spread her arms and wrapped them round me. 'Good girl,' she said. 'My little rebel. Maybe it will take a fight to get us out of this mess, but we must do something.' She smiled at me. 'You go and deliver the papers, love. I'm proud of you.'

Lily, whose ears had been wagging, said, 'Where's Daisy going?'

Mum reached out and pulled her on to her knee. 'Daisy's going to help someone,' she said. 'But we don't want to make Dad angry, so we must keep it a secret.'

'He won't be cross, will he, Mum?' she asked.

'Not if you keep the secret, Lily,' said Mum.

Lily sighed. 'Then I promise. I won't say a word.' And she pressed her finger to her lips.

Eighteen

I ran over to Arber's printing works and burst into the shop, where Mrs Stanbury was behind the counter as usual.

'I'm sorry, Mrs Stanbury,' I gasped. 'Mum can't come. Dad's making her work at home and look after the babies.'

'Oh dear. Is that what *she* wants, Daisy?'

I shook my head. 'No, it isn't. But things are really bad at home. Mum says if she works for the suffragettes it would only make things worse.'

'Of course,' said Mrs Stanbury. 'I understand.'

'But she said I could carry on delivering the papers – as long as we don't tell Dad. I think Mum's pleased I'm helping you. She said she was proud of me.'

Mrs Stanbury nodded her head. 'Of course she's proud of you. She's a good woman, your mother. She's just managing as best she can. There are a lot of women like that.' Then she smiled and said, 'Pick up your bag, Daisy, and do your paper round. I'll be here when you get back.'

I did the delivery much faster now that I knew the route. So I was back at the shop in no time. Mrs Stanbury made me a cup of tea and we chatted for a while. Then, just before I left, she gave me a handbill.

'Tuck this in your pocket,' she said. 'It's about the protest meeting on Sunday.'

'Oh, I read about that in the *Dreadnought*,' I said. 'I'd forgotten all about it.'

'You might want to go, Daisy,' she said, winking before she put tuppence into my hand.

'Thanks, Mrs Stanbury,' I said, and this time I ran home knowing that I could give the money to Mum as well as the other money I'd hidden away. It felt good.

Mum was really pleased when I handed her the pennies. 'Oh, that's grand. Thank you,' she said. 'You're a treasure, Daisy. But I'll have to be careful how I spend it or Dad will start asking where the money came from.'

'Will you buy me the blue dress, Mum?' asked Lily. 'I've been ever so good, haven't I?'

Mum laughed. 'Oh, what a little pickle you are, Lily. That blue dress will cost more than I have, I'm afraid.'

Lily's bottom lip began to tremble but, somehow, she managed to stop herself from bursting into tears. I gave her a hug and told her she was a brave girl.

'And now I must carry on stuffing these toy rabbits,' said Mum, pretending to be cheerful.

'I can give you a hand, Mum,' I said. 'Just show me what to do.'

'Me too,' said Lily.

Mum picked up the body of the rabbit and began

stuffing straw until it was nice and plump like a real rabbit. Then she shook her head. 'I'm not sure you should do it, girls.'

'Oh pleeeease, Mum,' said Lily. 'We can do it, can't we, Daisy?'

But when we tried, the straw hurt our fingers. Lily's hand started bleeding.

'You'll have to stop,' Mum said. 'I can't have you ruining your hands. Anyway, I think Dad will be pleased when he sees how many I've finished.'

We went and dipped our hands in the bucket and I wiped away the blood from Lily's palms. Her skin was softer than mine. The scratches made by the straw were deep and they must have hurt – but she never cried.

Later, when Dad walked in from work, Eddy and Frank were squealing and wriggling around on the rug and Mum was busy stuffing rabbits at the table.

'Well then,' he said, taking off his cap and hanging it on the hook. 'How are my girls today?'

'Mum's made a lot of rabbits, Dad,' said Lily as she grabbed hold of his hand. 'Come and see.'

She pulled him into the bedroom where Mum had put the finished rabbits – all thirty-two of them were spread out on the bed.

'The rabbits can't sleep here,' Lily explained. 'They have to go on the table when it's night-time. Mum said.'

Dad tickled her under her arm. 'Wouldn't you like to be in bed with lots of rabbits, Lily?' he asked.

'No. That's silly,' she said. 'There wouldn't be enough room for us.'

Dad laughed and walked back into the front room. 'Looks like you've done well, Florrie,' he said. 'How many does Mr Fredericks want?'

Mum kept her eyes on the rabbit she was stuffing. 'He said his best workers do sixty a day,' she said.

'Oh. Well, you're nowhere near sixty. You'd better get a move on then. You're not going to make much of a wage at this rate, that's for sure.'

Mum shut her eyes as though she wanted to block out his words. 'I can't work any faster,' she said, dropping the rabbit and holding up her hands. 'How can I work like this, Patrick? Just look at my hands.'

It was horrible to see. The skin was red and swollen, scratched from the straw and bleeding in places. They must have been so painful. Mum had been working hard from early this morning. No wonder her hands were in a terrible state.

Dad shrugged his shoulders. 'If you don't like it, you shouldn't have got yourself sacked, should you? Maybe the shirt factory wasn't as bad as you made it out to be.'

I could see Mum biting her bottom lip but she kept quiet.

'Now where's my tea?' Dad asked.

'There's some bread and cheese on the shelf,' she said.

Dad glared at her. 'Some men go home to a nice

stew, Florrie,' he said. 'You've been here all day, didn't you think of making a decent meal for your husband?'

'How could I?' Mum said, her voice hardly more than a whisper. 'We've no coal to do any cooking and I've no money to buy food.'

'You could have gone to the shop,' Dad said. 'Mrs Kaylock would put it on the slate.'

Mum shook her head wearily. 'Not any more. I owe too much. And word's probably got round that I lost my job. There's nothin' I can do, Patrick. Be thankful we've got bread and cheese.'

Her shoulders slumped as if she hadn't the energy to argue any more. Then tears spilled down her cheeks.

'Daisy,' said Dad. 'Go down to the pie shop and fetch a pie for tea, will you?' He dug his hand in his pocket and gave me a sixpenny bit and two pennies. 'That should be enough – so go sharpish and see what you can get.'

The pie shop was on the corner of Roman Road. There was often a queue of people waiting to be served, but that day the shop was empty when I arrived.

'Meat and potato pie, please,' I called to the man behind the counter. 'That one over there.' I pointed to a pie with a broken crust because I knew it would be cheaper than the others. Dad would be pleased I'd saved some money.

The man wrapped the pie in newspaper to keep it warm and I held it to my chest, hurrying home as fast as I could, not wanting it to get cold.

'I got it cheap, Dad,' I called out as I burst through the front door. 'Five pence.'

'Good girl,' he said, holding out his hand and pocketing the change. He took the pie and put it on the table before cutting it in half with a knife.

Dad had half the pie and left the other half for Mum, Lily and me.

'You've got the biggest piece, haven't you Dad?' said Lily.

'Course I have,' he said, his cheeks bulging as he ate. 'A man needs feeding, Lily. I'm the one who goes out to work, aren't I? Just remember that.'

I did remember that. It was one more thing that wasn't fair.

Nineteen

For the rest of the week, Mum wrapped rags round her hands to stop the pain and bleeding so that she could carry on stuffing toys. But even so, she found it more and more difficult, and she wouldn't let us help at all.

'If Mr Fredericks isn't pleased with me,' she said, 'then he'll have to find somebody who can work faster.'

We tried to help in other ways. When we came home from school, we went and filled the water bucket without being asked. Lily was really good at looking after Eddy and Frank and I went to the shop for bread and milk and, sometimes, cheese. Dad left money on the shelf every morning – but there was never enough, even with my pennies added to it.

On Sunday, Dad set off to take Great-Aunt Maude to Mass. But Mum looked exhausted after a whole week of stuffing rabbits.

'Will you two take the twins to the park this morning?' she said. 'I need a rest.' Of course we agreed. 'Have fun – but don't be too long, will you?'

When we arrived at Victoria Park, Eliza was already sitting in the shelter, and she waved as we walked towards her. It was a lovely warm day and Lily was bursting to go and paddle in the bathing pond.

'Could you look after Eddy?' she asked Eliza, who was only too pleased to take him and bounce him on her knee.

'Make sure you keep hold of your boots, Lily,' I said. 'Don't leave them on the grass, will you?'

While she was away, I asked Eliza about the jam factory. 'Did you get any more money this week?'

'A bit,' she said. 'But it's still awful work, Daisy. I'm worn out by the time I get home.'

Then I told her what had happened to Mum. 'Dad said she shouldn't have spoken to the boss like that, but she was just sticking up for a poor woman who was eating bread.'

'And she lost her job?' she said. 'That's so unfair.'

'I know,' I said, leaning closer. 'Can you keep a secret?'

'Course I can. Tell me.'

'I'm working for the suffragettes, delivering their newspaper.'

Eliza stared at me, her mouth open. 'Honest?'

'Yes, really. I get paid tuppence – but that's not why I do it. I think the suffragettes are trying to make things better. They say if we don't have the vote, we can't change the laws.'

'Does your dad know?' asked Eliza. 'He thinks them suffragettes are daft in the head, doesn't he? Most men do.'

I nodded. 'Yes, Dad would go mad if he found out I was doing something for them. But I don't care. I can't stand by and do nothing. I've even got a rosette that says "Votes for Women", but I hide it under the bed.'

We began to giggle at the thought of it and we couldn't stop for ages.

When we did, I told Eliza about the protest meeting at the Civic Hall. 'It's this afternoon,' I said. 'I'm going to go. Why don't you come too?'

'What would I have to do? I don't want to hit a policeman or go to prison. Nothing like that.'

'Neither do I,' I said. 'Mrs Stanbury said we'll be holding up banners and shouting "Votes for Women" – that kind of thing. Go on! Come with me. It's the only way things are ever going to change round here.'

'Is your mother coming?'

'I don't think so. She'll be stuffing toys. And Dad won't let her out of the house.'

Just then, Lily came running over the grass hugging her boots to her chest. The hem of her skirt was dripping wet.

'My legs are ever so clean, Daisy, and I looked after me boots like you told me to.' She held them out for me to see.

'Good girl,' I said, passing Frank over to Eliza. I squeezed as much water as I could out of Lily's skirt and then I rubbed her feet with my own petticoat.

'The sun will soon dry your skirt,' I said. 'Now, put your boots on, Lily. I think we should be going home.'

Just as we were about to leave, I tapped Eliza's shoulder. 'Remember what I said, won't you? The Civic Hall. Two o'clock.'

She wrinkled her nose. 'I'm not sure, Daisy. Maybe.'

Twenty

That dinnertime, when Dad came back from Great-Aunt Maude's, we cleared the table of rabbits and ate some bread and cheese together.

Lily chatted a lot about how Eddy was nearly crawling and how she was going to have a blue dress when she was grown up. Mum didn't say much and looked ever so pale.

When we'd all finished eating, Dad said, 'Right, I'm off to the Gunmaker's. I'd better be sharp. They close at three.'

'Can't you stay, Dad?' said Lily. 'You could tell us that story from when you and Mum were little in Ireland. Go on, I like that.'

'Not today, pickle,' he said ruffling her hair. Then he went into the bedroom and came out carrying a sack full of the rabbits Mum had made. 'I'm going to meet Mr Fredericks in the pub. He'll pay me for the rabbits.'

Mum looked up at him and her face clouded over and she pressed her lips together. She was angry and I knew why. She'd worked all week, but Dad was taking charge of the money.

He took his cap off the hook and put it on. 'I might be

back late. I've got to go to Tom's to collect my hammer.' With that, he walked out of the door.

We cleared the table and brought more rabbit pieces ready for Mum to stuff. But she pushed them away.

'I'm not doing any more. I can't.'

She rested her elbows on her knees and sank her face into her hands. It was some time before she lifted her head and spoke to us.

'I've turned into some kind of slave, haven't I? I don't even get to see the money I've earned.' She clenched her fist and squeezed her eyes shut. 'I won't go on like this. I won't!'

'Let's go for a walk, Mum,' I said. 'You'll feel better for some fresh air.'

Slowly and miserably, she nodded and stood up.

'Come on,' I said, taking her hand. 'I was planning on going out anyway.'

Mum was only half listening. 'Where to?'

'To the Civic Hall,' I said, giving her hand a tug. 'The suffragettes are holding a protest meeting. I think Eliza's going too. Why don't you come with us?'

'The suffragettes?' she said, as if she was too tired to remember.

'Yes, you know – Mrs Stanbury and Miss Pankhurst. They're holding a protest meeting,' I explained.

Then suddenly, Mum was wide awake. 'Well, I've got plenty to protest about, Daisy. I *will* come with you. Why not? Things can't get much worse, can they?'

I wasn't surprised that Lily didn't want to go with us. She wanted to stay at home and look after the twins, so Mum ran upstairs and asked Mrs Rosen to keep an eye on them.

'I'll stay on the doorstep with Alice,' Lily said. 'Eddy and Frank can sit on my knee and I'll watch the boys playing football.'

I went into the bedroom, pulled my suffragette rosette from its hiding place and pinned it on my dress. Mum put on her hat and gave Lily a hug.

'You're my good girl,' she said. 'Look after the twins for me and we'll be back soon. If Dad comes home, tell him I've gone for a walk with Daisy.'

As soon as we stepped outside, Mum looked better. Her eyes brightened and her cheeks flushed as she strode out along the street.

She smiled at me and said, 'You're looking very smart with your rosette, Daisy.'

I grinned.

'Now where did you say this meeting was?'

'The Civic Hall.'

'Oh, that's not far,' she said. 'It's a nice afternoon for a walk. The sun's shining and everything looks grand. Sure, it's just what I need. I'm glad you asked me.'

'Mrs Stanbury told me some Members of Parliament are talking in the hall.'

'Will we be going inside?'

'No. We'll be waiting for the MPs to come out and

we'll ask 'em why the government's not doing more about votes for women.' I grinned at Mum. 'But mostly we'll be shouting and waving banners.'

'Well, let's see what happens, shall we?' said Mum. 'It's about time women had their say.'

Twenty-one

The church clock struck two. We were almost at the Civic Hall when someone shouted, 'Daisy!' and I turned to see Eliza running towards us.

'I'm really glad you came,' I said when she got close. 'I wasn't sure you would.'

Mum was pleased to see her too. 'Hello, Eliza,' she said. 'Are you interested in the suffragettes then?'

'Not really, Mrs O'Doyle,' Eliza replied. 'But when Daisy told me about the meeting, I thought it sounded more exciting than staying at home.'

We walked on together. A few women had already gathered outside the Civic Hall, holding banners and placards that read 'Votes for Women' and 'Deeds Not Words'. They weren't making any fuss. They were just standing there quietly.

'They're waiting for the MPs to come out,' I said to Eliza. 'They'll want to ask 'em questions.'

'Are you going to ask one, Daisy?' Eliza asked.

'Don't be daft,' I said, nudging her with my elbow. 'I wouldn't dare, would you?'

'No!' she said, giggling. 'They'd all look at me. I'd be too embarrassed.'

As we waited, more women joined the group, some with their children, and I was amazed to see the crowd grow so big that I couldn't count everybody. This was fantastic!

Then, all of a sudden, one woman held a placard high in the air and called out, 'What are we waiting for, ladies?' Then she shouted, 'Votes for Women!'

Another one joined in. And another.

So I took a deep breath and shouted, 'Votes for Women!'

Then Eliza did too. 'Votes for Women!'

So did Mum. 'Votes for Women!'

It was like magic! What started with one voice spread until the whole crowd joined together, holding up their banners, waving and shouting, 'Votes for Women!' It was the most exciting thing I'd ever done.

Before long, the doors of the Civic Hall were thrown open and a man stepped out. He was very smart in a black suit with a waistcoat and a white shirt with a stiff collar.

'He must be one of the Members of Parliament,' said Mum. 'I don't know who he is.'

The man stood on the top step and held up his hand for quiet.

'Ladies!' he said. 'There is no need for this.'

Everybody stopped shouting and looked in his direction, waiting to hear what he had to say. The MP held up his chin, tucked his thumbs into his waistcoat and began to speak.

'I am your representative in the Houses of Parliament,' he said, puffing out his chest. 'The people inside the hall have come to hear me speak. But if you ladies carry on shouting, they won't be able to hear me.'

Then somebody yelled, 'What are you doing about women's suffrage?'

After that, everybody started shouting.

'We've got a right to have our say!'

'There ain't no women in Parliament. Why not?'

'We pay our taxes. Give us the vote!'

Even Mum pushed herself towards the front and shouted, 'What about women's rights at work?'

Everybody wanted their questions answered and they wouldn't be told to be quiet. Then two women ran up the steps of the Civic Hall waving a banner, but before they could reach the MP, he quickly turned and disappeared inside, slamming the doors behind him.

'Ain't it exciting, Eliza?' I laughed. 'I told you, didn't I? Glad you came now?'

'Yes, I am,' she yelled above the noise. 'Wait till I tell the girls at the factory.'

The street was now so tightly packed with the suffragettes, we were shoulder to shoulder. Then Eliza, who was looking behind us over the heads of the crowd, suddenly said, 'Oh blimey, Daisy. Look what's coming.'

'What is it? I can't see. I'm not as tall as you.'

'It's the bobbies. Loads of 'em. They've got truncheons.'

Suddenly, the women at the back of the crowd set off running down the road, but there was no escape. No side streets to hide down. All they could do was flatten themselves against the wall and hope the police would run past.

By then I was feeling scared. 'Can you see Mum, Eliza? Where is she?'

She craned her neck, looking around, but she couldn't spot her. 'She won't be far off,' she said. 'Don't worry.'

By then, everybody was panicking at the sight of the police. The women were pushing and jostling. Some were screaming – especially the young children, who must have been terrified.

Once the police had reached the Civic Hall, they formed a ring around the crowd to stop us running off. And then what followed was horrible. Some women started shouting at the police, jostling and complaining loudly, and then just as at Bow Baths, the police lashed out in every direction with their truncheons, hitting women and children alike, knocking them to the ground. I was so scared, I crouched down against the wall, shutting my eyes and covering my head with my hands, hoping it would all go away.

'Daisy!' yelled Eliza. 'Don't do that. Get up!' I felt her grab hold of my arm and drag me to my feet. 'Quick. Come on!'

My head was in a whirl. I couldn't think straight as I stumbled along, tugged by Eliza. I didn't know which way we were going or why. I don't know how we made it through the crowd, but we did. By the time my brain was working again, I realised Mum still wasn't with us.

'Where is she?' I screamed. 'I can't see her. Stop! We've got to find her.'

But Eliza wouldn't let go of my hand. 'Keep going, Daisy,' she said. 'She'll be all right. We'll find her later. We need to get away.'

Luckily, the police weren't interested in young girls. It was the grown-up suffragettes they were after. Maybe they thought Sylvia Pankhurst was in the crowd. But I knew she wasn't. Kosher Bill wasn't anywhere to be seen.

We hid around the corner of the Civic Hall. From there we could hear the footsteps of women running away. But – much worse – we heard screams and terrible cries as the police dragged off those who were left.

Terrified that Mum might be one of them, I crept to the corner of the building and peered round. Not far from the steps of the Civic Hall was a Black Maria with the back doors open. Two policemen were pulling a woman towards it, ignoring her cries as they flung her inside. Then I saw a terrible sight. A woman in a wheelchair was knocked over and left on the ground, unable to move, until a policeman dragged her like a sack of potatoes to the waiting van. Horrible! Horrible!

More and more women were taken. My heart was pounding furiously against my ribs. But I felt helpless.

What could I do? A girl like me against great strapping men? They grabbed another woman and I saw her struggle, kicking her legs, trying to tug herself free. She was doing everything she could not to give in. Scratching, biting, screaming. Near to the open doors of the van, she gave a final, courageous twist. That was when I saw her face. It was Mum. My mum was being dragged towards the Black Maria.

Now my own screams mixed with those of the women. I went wild. I would have flung myself at her attackers if Eliza hadn't stopped me. 'Don't, Daisy!' she said. 'If you go rushing out there, they'll arrest you too.'

Though I tried to break free of Eliza's grip, it was too late. The doors of the Black Maria slammed shut and I watched helplessly as it drove off.

'Where are they taking her?' I sobbed.

Eliza held me tight. 'Bow Police Station, I expect.'

Mum had been arrested and I didn't know what to do next.

My knees gave way and I sank to the ground.

Twenty-two

'I've got to go home,' I said once the road was clear. 'I've got to get my dad.'

Then I ran and ran, leaving Eliza behind. By the time I reached Tuttle Street I was scarlet-faced and gasping for breath, but nobody noticed. Mrs Pidgeon waved as she carried water from the standpipe, boys carried on kicking a ball around and Alice and Lily sat on the doorstep with the babies. Nothing had changed. But for me, my whole world had collapsed. Mum had been taken from us.

I pushed past Lily and ran into the front room where Dad was lolling in his chair, sleeping soundly.

'Dad!' I yelled. 'Dad! You've got to do something!'

He grunted but didn't wake so I shook him by the shoulder. 'Wake up, Dad! Please wake up!'

'What's the matter, Daisy?' asked Lily as she struggled inside with one twin under each arm. 'Why are you waking Dad?'

I prodded Dad again and this time his eyes rolled slowly open.

'What?' he said, still half asleep. 'What d'yer want?'

'It's Mum,' I said and Dad sat bolt upright.

'Where've you been, Daisy? Lily said you'd gone for a walk. Where's your mother? Why isn't she here?'

I took a deep breath, ready to tell him the truth, but terrified of what he would say.

'It's the coppers. They've arrested her.'

He stared at me as if he couldn't take in what I'd said.

'You've got to do something, Dad,' I said taking his hand and squeezing it. 'Go to Bow Police Station and get her out. You can do it, Dad. Please!'

'What's your mother done now, girl?' he said, reaching for his pipe. 'Got herself in trouble again?'

It was as if he hadn't heard me.

'She's been *arrested*, Dad. We were outside the Civic Hall at a suffragette meeting . . .'

He slammed his fist on the table so hard that his pipe bounced off and fell to the floor. Lily flinched and scuttled away with the twins into the bedroom.

'*Suffragettes?*' he roared. 'You mean she went to see them suffragettes again after I told her not to?' He banged his fist again. 'I told her! But she had to disobey me, didn't she? And now she's brought more shame on me.'

'She didn't do nothing wrong, Dad. It was just a meeting. But they arrested her.'

Dad groaned and held his head in his hands. 'My wife's been arrested!' he wailed.

'Yes, and she needs you, Dad!'

'What will they say at the factory when they hear,

eh?' he said, shaking his head from side to side. 'I was a laughing stock last week – and now this. I'm not master in my own house – that's what they'll say.'

'But Mum needs you,' I repeated. 'Please, Dad. Please go to the police station. They'll listen to you.'

Then he looked up at me, his eyes narrow and cold. 'No,' he said. 'This time she's gone too far with her troublemaking. They can lock her up for all I care. Maybe it'll teach her a lesson. I'm not going nowhere.'

I could hardly believe it. Dad was refusing to help. He was turning his back on our lovely mum who worked so hard for us.

Well! If Dad wouldn't do anything, I would. I couldn't stay at home while Mum was at the police station with nobody to speak for her. Without another word, I turned, ready to walk out.

'No you don't,' said Dad, grabbing me by the arm. 'You're stayin' here. You ain't going nowhere except to bed.'

'I will not!' I yelled. 'I'm going to help Mum.'

'You'll do as you're told, my girl,' he yelled. 'Or else!'

I shook myself free from his grip. But Dad was between me and the door. I couldn't escape. Near to tears, I ran into the bedroom where Lily was sitting on the floor with the twins.

'Why is Dad angry, Daisy?' she asked, her little face drawn with worry. 'Where's Mum?'

'Oh, he's just cross cos Mum and me went for a

walk,' I said. I didn't tell her the truth. I didn't want to upset her even more.

'Has Mum come home now?' she asked.

I shook my head. 'She had to stay a bit longer. She was talking to some friends,' I lied.

Time passed. We sat on the bed whispering to each other. I made up stories to take Lily's mind off things. She was worrying, I could tell. We were really hungry, but Dad didn't say anything about food and I didn't dare to ask.

As daylight faded, we lay on the bed and pulled the blankets over us.

We'd had nothing to eat and there was still no Mum.

Much later, when it was dark, Dad came and climbed into bed. Mum and Dad always slept at the top end and Lily and me at the bottom. But tonight there was just Dad in the bed and it felt strange. Lily held my hand and I heard her snuffling. Poor Lily. She was missing our Mum and I felt like crying too.

Twenty-three

I must have fallen asleep, because I was woken by someone knocking on the front door. Dad flung back the blanket and leaped out of bed, waking the twins who set off such a noise that it woke Lily too.

I scrambled out of bed and picked Frank out of the box.

'What's the matter?' moaned Lily, rubbing her eyes. 'Why are the babies crying?'

'Quick!' I said. 'Come and get Eddy. Dad's woken him up.'

While we rocked the twins and tried to get them back to sleep, we heard Dad drawing back the bolts and opening the front door.

'So it's you,' he said. 'You've finally come home, have you?'

I looked across at Lily, and we both smiled. Mum was back! We stood by the bedroom door, our ears pressed against the gaps in the wood, listening to what they said.

'I'm sorry, Patrick,' said Mum. 'I just went to a meeting . . .'

Dad didn't let her finish. 'I told you them suffragettes were no good,' he said. His voice was rough and angry.

'I told you to stay at home. You'd got work to do, hadn't you? But no! You knew better and you had to go and see them toffs with their fancy ideas.'

'Let me come in, Patrick,' Mum begged. 'Please!'

Her voice was so small and sad, I couldn't bear to hear it. She must have been so cold and frightened out there in the dark. Why wouldn't Dad let her in? Poor Lily was in a real state and looked like she was going to cry.

But Dad didn't seem bothered about upsetting us. He was really angry. Angrier than I'd ever known him.

'I'm ashamed of you, Florrie,' he yelled, loud enough to wake the whole street. 'You're a disgrace. A common criminal! I never thought you'd go around making trouble like this. You're not fit to be my wife any more, or a mother to my children. Go away! I won't have you in my house.'

He slammed the door shut and we could hear him sliding the bolts across, while Mum hammered on the door and called out, 'Patrick! Please! I'm sorry! Let me in!'

Our mum had always looked after us when we were upset, and now it was awful to hear her sound so scared.

I didn't think Dad would keep this up for long. I was sure he'd change his mind and let Mum in. But he didn't, and after a while, the knocking stopped. The twins finally stopped crying, then Lily and me tucked them back in their box and climbed into bed, clinging to each other. We were too scared to imagine what might happen next.

Not long after, a glimmer of candlelight crept through the cracks in the bedroom door and the smell of Dad's tobacco drifted in. I guessed he was sitting in his chair, smoking his pipe.

'Will Mum come back?' whispered Lily.

'I'm sure she will,' I said. 'Now we'd better go to sleep. You can see Mum in the morning.' I didn't know if this was true, but if it stopped Lily worrying, it was worth telling one small fib.

It must have worked, because she was soon asleep. I just lay there, listening for any noise in the other room, desperately hoping to hear the front door open or the sound of Mum's voice. Anything that told me Mum had come home. But there was nothing, apart from the creaking of the floorboards as Mrs Rosen moved about upstairs.

It was impossible for me to sleep. I snuggled up against Lily, still listening, until I heard the scrape of Dad's chair on the stone floor as he stood up. The candle was snuffed out and the bedroom door opened.

I stayed as still as I could, pretending to be asleep, as Dad climbed back into bed and pulled the blanket over him. I waited for a long time until he began to snore, then I breathed a sigh of relief. He was fast asleep and it was time for me to go and find Mum.

Slowly, I slid my legs out from under the blanket and dropped my feet on to the cold floor. Feeling my way in the dark, I crept around the bed, picked up my dress and pulled it on. Then I tucked my boots under my arm. In the front room, I groped around the table and over to the shelf where we kept the bread bin. I lifted the lid without a sound and found a good piece of bread in there. It was stale but if Mum was hungry she'd be glad of it. I was tempted to take a bite myself – but I didn't. Mum's need was greater than mine. I took her shawl off the hook by the door and wrapped the bread in it. Then I picked up my own shawl and covered my shoulders, knowing at that time of night, it would be cold.

Out in the side passage, I sat at the bottom of the stairs to the Rosens' rooms and put my boots on. As I fastened the buttons, I thought – so far, so good. I hadn't made any noise that might wake Dad. I hadn't knocked anything over and I hadn't tripped up. All I had to do now was get out of the front door.

I stood on tiptoe, reached for the top bolt and pulled it back.

I took hold of the door handle and turned it as Dad's snores grew louder than ever. He was so deeply asleep, he wouldn't know that I'd gone. If I made a run for it now, I was sure I'd be back before he woke up.

Outside, the street was dark as pitch. Even the moon was hiding behind a cloud. Which way should I go? I wondered. It was the middle of the night and I didn't know where Mum might be. I only knew that I had to find her.

Twenty-four

A bitter wind was blowing and I pulled my shawl tight around my shoulders. But the cold wasn't the worst of it. I'd never been out at that time of night. I was scared – afraid of being followed. There were no gas lamps in Tuttle Street and I was even frightened of meeting a ghost – which was daft because I didn't believe in ghosts.

I stood outside our door, waiting until my eyes got used to the dark, but when they did, Mum wasn't anywhere in our street. Why would she be? She'd want to get out of the cold. But I knew no one in Tuttle Street would take her in if they found out she'd been arrested. Maybe she'd gone to Mrs Stanbury's house. She'd help Mum, I knew she would. But Mrs Stanbury would have gone to bed hours ago and Mum wouldn't want to disturb her. She'd hate to be a nuisance.

I thought she might have gone to Saint Stephen's church. It wasn't far away. I'd heard that people went to churches when they were in trouble. Mum could have gone there.

So I hurried towards Mostyn Road and as I reached the church, the moon slid out from behind a cloud. Everything was washed in a ghostly light – including the churchyard. There stood dozens and dozens of gravestones, old and grey and crumbling. Just the sight of them gave me the collywobbles and I imagined dead bodies lying under the ground ready to leap out at me. If I hadn't thought Mum might be sheltering inside the church, I would never have gone within a mile of that graveyard. Never!

But I took a deep breath and charged down the path, not daring to look to the left or the right until I reached the porch over the church door. It was black as coal in there and it took some courage to step inside. I stretched my arms out in front of me and stepped slowly forward, one foot in front of the other, hoping I'd feel the handle on the church door.

That's when I tripped. *WHAM!* I fell forward and landed on something soft. Something that smelled of stale beer and dirty clothes. And a voice growled out of the dark, 'Geroff!'

I was terrified. And when a rough hand clutched my arm, I tried to pull away but another hand – just as rough – grabbed hold of my leg. 'Who are yer?' someone else said. 'What you doin' here?'

Those hands held me so tight that I wanted to scream with the pain of it. Instead, I stammered, 'I'm D . . . Daisy. Let me go! I'm looking for my mum.'

The body beneath me moved like a great whale. 'Oh, poor thing. Oh dear, oh dear,' mocked the first voice. 'She's looking for her mum, Edgar.'

Then the other voice chirped up again. 'Well, she ain't here,' he said, squeezing my ankle even tighter. 'This is our spot and we don't share it with nobody. SO HOP IT!'

He let go of me. Panic-stricken, I struggled to my feet and stood there, knowing that two men were sprawled between me and the church door. But now I'd come this far, I wasn't going to give up.

'What about the church?' I said. 'Can I go inside? Do you think my mum'll be in there?'

There was a burst of laughter followed by a lot of coughing, which ended with some stomach-churning spitting.

Once they'd finished making their revolting noises, one said, 'Do yer think we'd be out here, if that door was open, eh? Them vicars think we'll pinch their candlesticks if they don't lock it.' He leaned towards me and, although I couldn't see him, the stink of him made me feel ill. 'Now geroff or I'll give yer a thumpin'.'

I didn't need telling twice. I raced down the path so fast that I barely noticed the graves. When I reached the bottom of Mostyn Road, I leaned on the wall, gasping for breath and wondering where to go next.

It must have been the relief of escaping from the church – but an idea came in a flash. I don't know why I hadn't thought of it before. Mum would go to the shelter in the park. Of course she would! That was her favourite place and, providing no one had got there before her, she could sleep on the bench protected from the wind.

I raced along Old Ford Road and, once I'd reached the park, I could see the curved roof of the shelter in the distance with its white stone shining in the moonlight. I hadn't got far to go now and I knew Mum would be there. I just knew it.

There was an old oak tree a few feet from the shelter. When I reached it, I leaned against it and closed my eyes, getting my breath back. But if I'm honest, I'd lost my nerve. I was so scared, I hardly dared look into the shelter. What if Mum wasn't there? I couldn't bear it. Where would I look next?

Instead of opening my eyes and going to look, I said, 'Mum!' That's all I said. 'Mum!'

I didn't move. With my eyes still closed, I clung to the tree, hoping she would come to me. Hoping she would say everything was all right. I waited with my fingers digging into the rough bark of the oak, listening to the rustle of the leaves. I felt my heart racing as if it was fit to burst.

She didn't come. But when I opened my eyes I saw something move in the shadow of the shelter.

'Mum!' I called again as tears welled up and spilled down my cheeks.

Then I heard it. It was almost a whisper. 'Daisy?' And my heart stopped. My legs felt weak and I wanted the ground to swallow me up. Surely that voice was just in my head. But I desperately wanted it to be real. 'Please let it be real,' I said to myself.

'Daisy!' The voice was louder now and as I stared at the shelter, Mum came tumbling out, stiff from the cold.

'Daisy, my girl,' she cried, spreading her arms wide and gathering me up. 'You shouldn't be out at this hour. But oh! It's grand to see you.'

Her hands and cheeks were ice-cold, but it was so good to feel her arms round me that nothing else mattered.

Twenty-five

We sat close together on the bench in the shelter. Mum was glad of the shawl and the bread I'd brought her.

'That was kind of you, Daisy, but you know your dad will be angry that you've come looking for me.'

'He won't know. Honest, Mum. He was snoring really loud when I left. He won't wake up till morning.' Then I suddenly felt near to tears. 'This is all my fault.'

'Nonsense,' said Mum. 'Why do you think that, darlin'?'

'Cos I told you about the meeting, and I asked you to go with me.'

'But I wanted to go, and do you know, I'm glad I did. Yes, I got arrested – and that was horrible. But for once I felt I was fighting to change things, that I was with people who knew how to make that happen – if only men would listen.'

I squeezed her hand.

'Now I want you to go home, Daisy. No need for us both to be out here.'

'I'm not going, Mum,' I said. 'Not till you've told me what happened at the police station.'

She sighed and nodded. 'All right then. If I must . . . Well, it wasn't very nice, that's for sure. They bullied all of us, Daisy, and they flung us into cells. We were left there for hours, and then they questioned us one at a time. Some of the women were charged with disturbing the peace and packed off to Holloway. I was really scared I'd be sent there as well.'

'But you weren't, were you?' I said.

Mum shook her head. 'They didn't think I was very important. They said they were giving me a warning but the next time I got into trouble, I'd be in Holloway too. After, they let me go and I had to walk home.'

I gave her a big squeeze. 'You must have felt awful, Mum!' I said. 'And then Dad wouldn't let you in.'

'I wasn't surprised,' she said. 'Your dad has a bit of a temper sometimes. But it doesn't last long. He thinks I've shown him up and he's embarrassed, but I expect he'll have calmed down by tomorrow.'

'So what are you going to do?'

'I'll come home and talk to him when he gets back from the factory,' she said. 'Everything will be back to normal, you'll see. Now get off sharpish or I shall worry about you, Daisy.'

I stood up ready to leave, but first I said, 'Go and see Mrs Stanbury in the morning, Mum. Please. She's at Arber's printing works in Roman Road. She'll give you a cup of tea and something to eat. And a job if you want it. Promise me you will. Promise!'

Mum agreed that she would go and I hugged her before I set off running back home.

Twenty-six

I slept well for the rest of the night and was woken by the slamming of the front door. Dad had gone to work without waking us up, without saying a word. That was mean. He was obviously still in a bad temper.

I shook Lily's shoulder. 'We've got to get up. Quick!' I said. 'The twins will need feeding.'

Lily opened her eyes, which were still a bit swollen from crying. 'Is Mum home?' she asked.

I shook my head and said, 'I expect she'll be here when we get back from school, Lily. Come on. We've got things to do.'

We climbed out of bed, pulled our dresses over our petticoats and slipped on our boots.

'Ouch!' cried Lily.

'What's the matter?'

'My toes hurt,' she said, pushing out her bottom lip. 'These boots are too small. I keep telling Dad that I need some new ones but he just forgets.'

I thought she was going to cry. 'Well, I'll ask him when he comes home from work, Lily. I promise.'

That made her feel better, though deep down I didn't think Dad had the money for another pair – even second-hand boots cost a lot. If her feet kept growing, she might have to go without – which would be all right in summer but not so good when the weather got cold. Plenty of kids in Bow went barefoot. I suppose they just got used to it.

'What about the twins, Daisy?' Lily asked. 'Who's going to look after them if Mum's not here?'

I knew Dad would expect me to stay at home but I wasn't going to. I was going to school whatever happened.

'We'll take 'em to Mrs Griggs,' I said. 'I don't suppose she'll be very pleased, but it's the best we can do.'

I was right. As we walked up Tuttle Street carrying the twins, Mrs Griggs was standing on the doorstep, her arms folded across her chest.

'Well, I can't say I'm surprised to see you two,' she sneered. 'Your mum and dad woke the whole neighbourhood last night with their shouting. Your mum's made a fool of herself getting mixed up with them suffragettes. She got arrested, didn't she?'

I was flabbergasted and *angry*! What a nosey old woman. 'How did you know that?' I said.

A nasty smirk spread across her face. 'The whole street knows about it. By the end of the day, the whole of Bow will know about it. We don't think much of them suffragettes round here. I'm surprised your mother's taken up with 'em. I'd have thought she'd know better.'

We stood there, our mouths hanging open. To think that someone was talking about our mum like that!

'I suppose you want me to look after your little brothers, do you?'

We nodded nervously.

'Well, I won't see 'em suffer just because your mum doesn't know how to behave. You'd better give 'em here,' Mrs Griggs said, holding out her hands.

I was shocked that our family was the talk of Bow. How could that happen? My throat had tightened so much that I couldn't speak as we passed the twins over to her.

'I'll need paying, remember,' she shouted down the street as we ran away as fast as we could.

At school that day, I found it hard to concentrate on my work. Everybody was talking about me and whispering behind my back, but I didn't care. I could only think about Mum and hope she had gone to see Mrs Stanbury. Most of all, I wondered if she would make up the quarrel with Dad tonight. All these things were going round and round in my head and I was glad when lessons were finished for the day.

When we went to pick up the twins, Mrs Griggs was furious because we had no money.

'Sorry, Mrs Griggs,' I said as we grabbed hold of Eddy and Frank. 'Dad left for work without leaving us any. Thanks for looking after 'em.'

Then we ran away down the street with Mrs Griggs

yelling, 'You tell your dad when he comes home – I want paying.'

When we arrived at number 34, Alice Rosen was sitting on the step as usual.

'My mum's not very pleased with your mum,' she sneered. 'All that yelling and hammering on the door last night. She woke us all up, she did. Ought to be ashamed of herself. She was taken to the police station, wasn't she?'

With our mouths tight shut, we managed to push past her, bumping into her accidentally-on-purpose and standing on her bare toes. Alice howled in pain but we took no notice. That'll teach her to keep her nose out of our business, I thought.

Once we were inside our house, we needed to feed the twins. I picked up the milk jug but it was empty. We'd given them the last drop that morning. And there was no bread. I reached for the little blue tin on the shelf where Mum kept her money and I tipped it out into my hand. There were five pennies.

'I'm going to fetch some bread and milk,' I told Lily and I ran down to the shop, carrying the empty milk jug with me.

As I pushed the shop door open, the bell jangled letting Mrs Kaylock know that she had a customer.

'Hello, Daisy love,' she said walking out of the room at the back. 'What can I do for you?'

'Can I have some milk and some bread, Mrs Kaylock, please?' I said as polite as I could.

'Have you got the money, Daisy?' she asked. 'Only you know I can't let you have any more on tick. Your mum still owes me quite a bit.'

My cheeks were burning hot with embarrassment as I held out my hand and showed her the coins. 'Is that enough, Mrs Kaylock?' I asked.

She smiled at me. 'It is, love,' she said. 'I think you could afford a bit of cheese too. Would you like that?'

I hadn't expected Mrs Kaylock to be so kind and I nodded eagerly, thinking of my poor stomach, which had been empty all day.

She took the jug and went round the back to fill it up. She lifted a loaf off the shelf and put it on the counter. Then she turned to a large slab of cheese, picked up the cutting wire and sliced a good piece off it. I didn't think I could afford such a big piece and I could hardly stop my mouth from watering at the sight of it.

'There you are, Daisy,' she said as she wrapped the cheese in paper. 'You enjoy that.' Then, to my surprise, she leaned over the counter and said in a low voice, 'I was sorry to hear about your mother's trouble, Daisy. She's a good woman. I hope it will be sorted soon.'

I thanked her and set off home, clutching the bread and cheese in my left arm and holding the milk jug very carefully in my right hand to make sure I didn't spill a single drop.

Once we'd fed the boys, I cut some cheese and some

slices of bread for Lily and me. We deserved it and we were too hungry to wait till Dad came back.

'I've got to deliver the papers now, Lily,' I said when we'd finished. 'Remember, it's a secret.'

'I won't tell nobody, Daisy,' she said, pressing her finger to her lips. ''Specially not Dad.'

'Good girl. And will you go up and tell Mrs Rosen I've had to go out and you'll be looking after the twins?'

'Yes, I will. I can do that. I'm six now.'

I set off for Arber's printing works, desperately hoping Mum would be there.

Twenty-seven

When I arrived, Mrs Stanbury was in the shop stacking handbills on the counter.

'Hello, Daisy,' she said. 'The papers are in the bag for you. They're all ready.'

I was disappointed not to see Mum, but then Mrs Stanbury opened the door that led into the back room and called, 'Mrs O'Doyle. There's someone here to see you.'

My heart beat so fast, I thought it would burst as Mum came hurrying into the shop wearing a large ink-stained apron. 'Daisy!' she said, her face breaking into a great big smile. 'Oh, it's so good to see you.' And she gave me a huge hug, which meant I got splodges of ink on my face – but I didn't care.

'I did what I promised, Daisy,' Mum said. 'I came round here this morning and Mrs Stanbury has looked after me – just like you said.'

'I had to make her an extra-strong cup of tea when she arrived,' said Mrs Stanbury. 'She was cold to her bones after a night out in the park. I told her, she should have come round to my house. She could have had a bed for the night.'

Mum smiled. 'You've been very kind, Mrs Stanbury, and that cuppa did the trick. Thank you.'

'Your mum's been really useful to me all day,' Mrs Stanbury said. 'I don't know how I'd have got things done if she hadn't been here.'

It turned out that Mum had helped with sorting the pages of this week's *Dreadnought* and watching over the printing machine.

'I've enjoyed it,' Mum said. 'Though you can see it's a bit messy. I just wish I could read what they're printing. I'm sure it's all very clever and makes a lot of sense.'

'There are plenty who'll teach you to read,' said Mrs Stanbury. 'You're a clever woman, Mrs O'Doyle. You'll soon learn.'

Mrs Stanbury made us a cup of tea and all we chatted for a while until I said, 'I think I'd better go and deliver the papers now. I don't want to be late back.'

Before I left, Mum told me she'd come home and talk to Dad later that day. 'Don't you worry, my lovely Daisy,' she said. 'Dad's tempers never last long. I'll be home to look after you before you know it.'

I did the paper round in double-quick time. I couldn't wait to tell Lily that I'd seen Mum.

Back at home, Lily and me tidied up the front room and played with the twins while we waited for Dad. We waited ages but he didn't come. We were wondering where he was and getting a bit worried, when suddenly there was a knock on the door.

A chill ran up my spine. That couldn't be Dad. He wouldn't knock. He'd walk straight in. I thought the worst. Something bad had happened. He'd had an accident at the factory or he'd been taken ill.

I ran to the door and flung it open. But it wasn't somebody from the factory, it was Mum. She was standing there, looking pale and worried.

'I've come to speak to your dad, Daisy,' she said. 'Will he talk to me, do you think?'

I shook my head. 'He's not home from work, Mum. I don't know where he is.'

Mum lowered her chin. 'Oh dear,' she said, looking miserable and lost. 'I need to speak to him, don't I? I don't know what to do.'

I took hold of her hand. 'I think you should come in,' I said, tugging her inside. 'You need to sit down, Mum.'

When Lily saw Mum she bubbled over with excitement. Mum sat on the chair and pulled Lily on to her knee.

'Where have you been, Mum?' she asked and kissed her cheek over and over.

Mum said, 'I'm sorry I wasn't at home last night, Lily. But you were a good girl, weren't you?' And Lily nodded. 'And how have the boys been?'

Eddy and Frank were on the rug and Mum knelt down to pick them up.

'Oh, I'll swear they've grown since yesterday,' she

laughed and jiggled them up and down, which made them squeal with laughter and made us all feel happier.

Then Dad arrived.

When he saw Mum, his face flushed red. 'You!' he said, glaring at her. 'What d'you think you're doing in my house? I told you to leave, didn't I? You're no wife of mine.'

As he stepped into the room, I saw that he wasn't alone. There was somebody behind him. My stomach knotted when I saw that it was Great-Aunt Maude, as grim as ever in her black straw hat and her old black coat.

Mum, still holding the twins, was near to tears. 'I'm sorry, Patrick,' she said. 'I know I've upset and embarrassed you, but we can put all that behind us, can't we? I want to come back to my family.'

Great-Aunt Maude stood glowering at Mum. 'You should have thought of your family before you went stirring up trouble at the factory,' she said.

'I . . . I didn't go stirring up trouble,' said Mum nervously.

Great-Aunt Maude screwed up her face, tapping her stick on the flagstone floor as she moved closer to Mum. 'The whole of Bow knows you've been mixing with them suffragettes and getting yourself arrested. You can't expect a man to put up with the shame of that.'

'That's right,' said Dad. 'And I won't put up with it. So you can leave right now. Aunt Maude will be moving in to look after the kids.'

Mum went white with shock.

'But . . . but I can't leave my family,' she stammered, tightening her grip on the babies.

'Family?' yelled Dad. 'You've got no family now. You're not a wife and you're not a mother. I'm the man of this house and these children belong to me. That's the law, Florrie. And I'm afraid you and your suffragette friends won't change that.' Then he snatched the twins out of her hands and passed them to Great-Aunt Maude. 'You're on yer own. You made your choice. Now go!'

By then, Eddy and Frank were screaming fit to lift off the roof. Lily was yelling and tugging at Dad's trouser leg and I was shouting, 'No, Dad. You can't do that. We want Mum to come back. Please.'

But Dad took no notice of any of us. Instead, he grabbed hold of Mum's arm, dragged her to the door and pushed her out into the street.

Twenty-eight

After Mum left, the space in the middle of the bed was taken up by Great-Aunt Maude, who was old and smelled of mothballs. Her feet were the worst part of her. They poked down towards our end of the bed, stinking of cesspits, and the only way we could get to sleep was to pinch our noses tight.

Dad must have slept in his chair in the front room, but I couldn't be sure because he was gone by the time we got up in the morning.

Once we were dressed we found Great-Aunt Maude feeding the boys. She was really nice to them, but she did nothing but bark orders at Lily and me.

'Fetch some water and be sharp about it.'

'Cut some bread.'

'No, not that much. That's a doorstop. Here, give me the knife.'

'Off you go to school, sharpish.'

'You'll scrub this floor when you get back.'

Great-Aunt Maude was so different from Mum. Chalk and cheese they were. Mum was funny and kind – always smiling. Great-Aunt Maude almost never smiled. Not that I wanted her to. She had lost every tooth in her head except for two in the middle of the bottom row. Whenever I saw those teeth, they reminded me of a bulldog I knew.

That day, we set off for school leaving her fussing over Eddy and Frank. I think she liked babies. She definitely didn't like us, so we were glad to get out of the house.

School was worse than ever because, by then, everybody knew what had happened. The news had spread like wildfire round Bow – but not all of it was true. Some had heard Mum chained herself to the gates of Buckingham Palace. Others said she'd put a bomb in a pillar box and blown it up. And most said she was locked up in Holloway Prison and would be there for years.

It was ridiculous.

I told 'em straight that these stories were rubbish and most of the girls in my class believed me. Most of them. Not all.

When I was out in the schoolyard, three girls started marching in a line, their arms round each other's shoulders, chanting, 'Daisy's mum is a crazy suffragette,' over and over. They thought it was hilarious but I didn't. I went wild and charged over to them, fists clenched at the ready. It was only Miss Spike stopping me that saved 'em from black eyes and bloody noses.

What surprised me most though was that Miss Spike didn't make me write a thousand lines of 'I must control my temper' as she normally would. That made me think that she knew how bad things were at home and why I was finding it hard to do my work. Maybe I was wrong about her. Maybe deep down, she wasn't nearly as bad as I'd thought. Or maybe she was a secret suffragette too!

When school finished and I was walking out of the school gates with Lily, we were in for a surprise. A nice surprise. The kind of surprise I could never have dreamed of. There was Mum, waiting for us. How amazing was that?

Lily ran towards her. 'Mum! Mum!' she yelled and flung herself at her, taking her breath away.

'Mrs Stanbury said I could come to see you,' she said, when she broke free. 'She's been so kind. I've been working at Arber's all day and I've been longing to see you two.'

She asked how the twins were.

'Great-Aunt Maude makes a real fuss of them, Mum,' I said.

Then Lily added, 'But she's got terrible smelly feet and she's always shouting at us. I don't like her, do you, Daisy?'

'Now, now,' said Mum. 'She'll be looking after you until I come back home.'

'Will you be home soon?' asked Lily.

'I hope so,' said Mum. 'Now shall we go for a walk and you can tell me what you've been doing at school?'

It was so good to be with Mum, walking across the

park. She told us that she found the work at Arber's very interesting. 'It's so much better than stuffing rabbits,' she said and we all giggled. 'Mrs Stanbury's helping me with my reading and she said I can stay at her house until I go back home.'

'That's good, Mum,' I said. 'I didn't like you sleeping in the park. There's some bad people about.' I remembered the two men in the church porch and I shivered.

It was so good to be together again, but when it was time to go home, Lily got all weepy and clung to Mum.

'I'll come and see you tomorrow,' Mum said, giving her a big hug. 'But you mustn't tell Great-Aunt Maude. Can you do that, Lily?'

'Is it another secret?' she asked, her eyes full of tears.

Mum kissed her all over her cheeks and said, 'Yes, it's an important secret.'

And my little sister nodded seriously.

'Take care of the four of you, Daisy,' she said as she hugged me.

Before we parted, I whispered, 'Will you tell Mrs Stanbury I won't be able to deliver the newspapers now? I don't think Great-Aunt Maude will let me out.'

Mum nodded and we went our separate ways – we headed for Tuttle Street and Mum went back to Arber's.

Twenty-nine

Great-Aunt Maude was feeding the twins when we arrived home. They seemed very happy, kicking their little legs and laughing. She was really nice to the boys. But she was different with us.

'Where've you been?' she called over her shoulder as I walked in. 'Fetch some water, girl, and scrub this floor. It's a disgrace.'

I stared at her, shocked at the way she spoke to me.

'Get a move on,' she snapped, before turning to Lily. 'There's a chamber pot needs emptying, young lady. Take it to the privy – and make sure you don't spill any on the way. And when you come back you can wash that filthy window. It looks as though it ain't been cleaned since King George were a lad.'

These jobs took us some time. Poor Lily had never cleaned a window and she was very slow. By the time we'd finished, Dad was back from work. There was no smile on his face. In fact, he looked exhausted.

'The boys are tucked up, nice and neat, Patrick,' said Great-Aunt Maude as Dad slumped into his chair. 'I've got plenty of bread and cheese for your tea.' She spoke as if she'd gone shopping and carried it back herself. It was the same bread and cheese I'd got from Mrs Kaylock the day before.

Dad looked at the cheese. 'I'm not hungry,' he said, pushing it away. 'I think I'll go over to the Gunmaker's Arms for a bit. I've had a hard day.'

'You go, Patrick,' she said. 'Don't bother about me. I'll manage.'

I could tell from her smarmy voice that she was trying to wheedle something out of him.

'I wonder if you'd be so kind as to bring me a jug of ale when you come back, Patrick. As much as I love looking after them boys, it's terrible thirsty work.'

Dad didn't look pleased. 'Daisy,' he sighed. 'Fetch a jug and come with me.'

'Oh, that's very thoughtful of you,' said Great-Aunt Maude, trying to be pleasant, her two teeth on full display. 'You enjoy your evening with your pals, Patrick, and Daisy here will carry the ale back.'

Dad looked sharply at her. 'Don't get used to it, Auntie. I can't afford to go buying you beer every day.'

He walked out of the door while I reached for the jug off the shelf.

Once Dad was out of earshot, Great-Aunt Maude lost her smile. 'You be careful when you come back, my girl. Spill one drop and you'll know about it.' And she pinched my arm hard.

As we walked towards the Gunmaker's Arms, Dad asked, 'Are you behaving yourself for your Great-Aunt Maude?'

'Yes, Dad,' I said. I didn't like to mention that she was mean and took up a lot of space in the bed and that, more than anything, we wanted her to go and for Mum to come back.

I was surprised when he said, 'I don't suppose you know where your mum's gone?'

'No,' I lied. 'I'm sure she's all right. But I think she misses being at home.'

Dad stopped and stared at me, his eyebrows raised. 'Why do you think that? Have you spoken to her, Daisy?'

I really didn't like to fib but I had to. If I told him I'd seen her and that she was working with the suffragettes, there'd be another terrible row. Better to let things settle down for a few days. 'No, Dad,' I lied. 'I haven't spoken to her.'

He set off walking at a faster pace, looking ever so angry. 'She'd rather be with them suffragette women than be with her own family,' he said, as if he was talking to himself. Then he shook his head. 'I can't understand it, Daisy. She's changed and I don't know what they've gone and put into her head.'

Before he'd worked himself up into a frenzy, we reached the Gunmaker's Arms. Dad went inside, taking the jug with him, and in a couple of minutes he brought it out filled with beer.

'You take this home, Daisy. I'll be back later.'

When I got home, Great-Aunt Maude took the jug from me without so much as a thank you. She settled down at the table and poured herself a mug full of ale, which she emptied down her throat in no time.

'Go to bed, you two,' she snapped as she filled the mug again. 'Give me some peace and quiet. I've been on me poor legs all day.'

We'd been in bed for some time when Great-Aunt Maude came staggering into the bedroom and lurched on to the bed. We quickly pulled our legs out of the way so she wouldn't squash them. The stink of beer was on her breath, which mixed horribly with the stench of her feet. And her snoring kept us awake for ages.

The next night, Great-Aunt Maude asked, 'What about my beer, Patrick? Shall Daisy come with a jug?'

'I've no money for beer,' Dad told her. 'And I'm not going to the Gunmaker's any more. Nobody said a word to me yesterday, let alone bought me a pint. So you won't be getting any, Aunt Maude. The money I've got goes to pay for food – just you remember that.'

After that, Dad took to going out every evening when he'd had his tea. If he wasn't going to the Gunmaker's, we weren't really sure where he was going – and we didn't want to ask him. But what Dad didn't know was that, once he'd gone out, Great-Aunt Maude took coins from the little blue tin. That money was meant for bread and milk – and an egg if there was enough. But she used most of it for her beer. What a nerve! Every night, she threatened me with her stick if I didn't go to the Gunmaker's to get it and she made sure she'd drunk it before Dad came back. I hated her for that.

The only good thing about her was that as long as she was staying with us, she could look after Eddy and Frank and I could go to school. But if Mum stayed away much longer, I was worried that Dad would make me leave. My dream of being a nurse was looking much less likely now.

But Great-Aunt Maude was always moaning at us. Every day she grumbled about something. She even told us we took up too much room in the bed.

'You keep me awake with your wriggling,' she grumbled. 'And I need my sleep, I do. I'm exhausted with looking after the little 'uns all day. You'll have to sleep on the floor.'

The bed took up most of the space in the room. The only place for us to sleep was among the dust and the cobwebs under the bed. That's where we had to lie, curled up with a blanket over us. It wasn't comfortable on the hard floor, but at least we couldn't smell her feet.

We did get our own back though. One day, we collected some nice black cockroaches, which regularly ran across the floor, and we put them in the bed. We waited for Great-Aunt Maude to come in and held our breath while she climbed into bed and then . . . AAARRGGHHHHH! She jumped about screaming blue murder, batting the beetles with her shoe, *BANG! BANG! BANG!* until they were squashed flat in a black mess on the mattress.

It was the best bit of fun we'd had for days.

Thirty

After school on the following Wednesday, Mum was waiting for us at the gate. Seeing her made us so happy but saying goodbye was really hard. I felt like I was being torn apart, and Lily was getting more and more upset. Then on Thursday as we walked round the park, Lily couldn't hold back the tears. 'When are you coming back, Mum? Please come back. Please, please! We'll be ever so good. I promise.'

Mum tried to smile but I could see she was upset too. 'Not long now, Lily,' she said. 'I'll come and talk to Dad again on Sunday. Is he still angry with me, do you think?'

I told her that we didn't see much of him.

'He won't talk to us,' Lily sobbed. 'He goes out when he's had his tea and he don't come home till late.'

It wasn't easy for Mum to hear this, so I tried to cheer her up by telling her how well I was doing at school.

'Miss Spike thinks I'm brilliant,' I said. 'I'm top of the class in writing and sums now. I'm working really hard.' This wasn't exactly true as my brain had been muddled ever since Mum left. But still, one little fib made her smile and that was good enough for me.

'You don't think Dad's going to make me leave school, do you?' I asked.

'I really don't know,' said Mum. 'Money's tight and he's got a lot of mouths to feed.'

Every day we'd spend half an hour – maybe a whole hour – with Mum. It was easy to meet after school because Great-Aunt Maude didn't know what time we were let out.

But then she found out.

It happened on Thursday when Tommy Watkins called at our house.

'Is Daisy in?' he'd asked.

She'd said I was still at school.

Then he told her that school had finished nearly an hour ago.

He didn't mean to get me into trouble, but that's how it started.

When we arrived back home that day, Great-Aunt Maude was standing outside, her eyes squeezed narrow and mean like a wild cat ready to pounce.

'Get in!' she shrieked, waving her walking stick above her head. 'Get in this minute!' As we dashed past her into the house, she tried to whack us with the stick – but we were moving so fast that she missed and almost fell flat on her face.

Once she'd recovered, she staggered inside and flopped on to a chair, breathless, while we stood still, wondering what had made her so angry. Lily was already shaking and I held her hand tight to calm her down.

'Where've you been?' the old woman snapped, her voice as mean as a rattlesnake. 'Don't just stand there. I know you've been up to something. What have you been doing since you came out of school, eh?'

When we didn't reply, she raised her stick and thwacked it down on the table, making us both jump. She did that again so hard that I thought the stick was sure to break. Poor Lily was in tears. I had to say something.

'It was my fault,' I said, lowering my chin. 'I was fooling around in class and Miss Spike kept me in.'

'Fooling around?' she growled and rose to her feet. 'Fooling around? Then I'll have to teach you how to behave proper, won't I, eh?'

'Yes, I'm sorry,' I said meekly, thinking that an apology would be enough. But it wasn't.

'Oh yes, you'll be sorry, my girl. Now you'll get what's coming to you.'

Before I could say another word, she grabbed my arm and dragged me to the nearest chair.

'Bend over!' she snapped.

I did as she told me, clinging on to the chair, imagining the worst. Out of the corner of my eye, I saw her reach for the wooden spoon Mum kept in an old jar and used for cooking.

'Now see if this'll teach you,' she muttered.

Quickly, she pulled up my skirt and *THWACK!* – she brought the spoon down hard on my bare legs and

I screamed. I shouldn't have screamed. I knew it would frighten Lily, but the pain took my breath away. Mum had never beaten me and neither had Dad. *THWACK!* Again the spoon cracked across my legs. Again I cried out. *THWACK!* Again and again.

'No!' shrieked Lily, flinging herself at Great-Aunt Maude. 'Stop it!' she sobbed. 'Daisy was telling a lie. She didn't have to stay in after school. We went for a walk with Mum, that's all.'

Great-Aunt Maude turned, panting from the effort of the beating. Lily sank to the floor in floods of tears and I stood up from the chair, my legs throbbing.

'So,' Great-Aunt Maude said, slapping the spoon on the palm of her left hand. 'You're a liar, are you, Daisy O'Doyle? Well, from now on, you'll not be seeing your mother no more. Do you hear me?'

Lily howled but I just gritted my teeth.

'How many times have you been and met her?' she asked.

'I don't know,' I muttered.

The old woman's face twisted into a smirk. 'Don't know? Well I'm guessing it was three times. Am I right?'

I didn't speak.

'So I'll double it up for lying. You'll have six strikes, my girl.'

Six more strikes! The thought of them was terrifying. I didn't know how I could bear more pain. But the nasty old woman hadn't finished.

'And then,' she said, 'for going to see your mother . . .
I'll give your Lily six strikes as well. She's not too young to
learn.'

That did it! 'You won't touch my sister!' I yelled,
suddenly filled with uncontrollable rage. 'You won't
touch me either.' Then I snatched the spoon out of her
hand.

I think she was shocked that I had dared to answer
her back. Her mouth dropped open and she sank on to
the chair, staring at me.

When she spoke, her voice was weak and quaking.
'I'll tell your father you've been meeting your mother.
Don't be surprised, missy, if he takes his belt off to yer.'

'No he won't! Our dad ain't never hit us. Never!'

I was so angry that I began to shake. Great-Aunt
Maude wasn't going to get the better of me. I was
younger and smaller than she was, but I was determined
to stand up to her.

'When Dad comes home tonight,' I shouted, 'I'll tell
him how you steal money out of the tin. How you make
me get beer for you and how you get drunk every night.'

'You stupid girl,' she growled. 'You wouldn't dare.'

'Oh, wouldn't I? Just wait and see.'

Her face turned purple with fury and she snatched
up her walking stick. Looking like a mad old witch, she
raised it up high and flung it at me. Thank goodness it
missed Lily but it cracked me on the shoulder, knocking
me off balance so that I landed face down on the floor.

Blood spurted from my nose and when I pulled myself upright, pain shot through my knee so bad that I thought I would faint.

I just stood there, breathing deeply. Furious.

'We're not staying here,' I said, taking hold of Lily's hand. 'We're going.'

Thirty-one

In spite of the terrible pain in my knee, I managed to limp away fast. I don't know how I did it – I think I was so desperate to get away from Great-Aunt Maude that I was able to ignore it. We went to the only place I knew where we'd get help: Arber's printing works. By the time we reached Roman Road, I was in agony and Lily was crying her heart out.

'Mrs Stanbury!' I shouted as I flung open the door of the shop. 'Mrs Stanbury! You've got to help us. Please.'

She hurried out from behind the counter and put her arm round my shoulder to help me hobble inside. 'Whatever's the matter?' she said. But before we could answer, Mum came rushing from the back room into the shop.

'Oh, Daisy . . . Lily . . . what is it?' she asked. 'What's happened?'

I was leaning on the counter and I suppose my face looked a mess. Blood was running from my nose and my right eye was beginning to swell. Mum was all of a tizzy.

'Help Daisy into the back room, Florrie, and sit yourselves down,' said Mrs Stanbury. 'I'll find a clean rag for her face then I'll make a pot of tea. Don't you worry, girls. You're safe here.'

Mum cleaned the blood off my face and then she lifted Lily on to her knee while I explained what had happened.

'It was horrible,' sobbed Lily. 'Great-Aunt Maude is a witch!'

Mum sat there shaking her head, near to tears. 'I'm so sorry,' she said. 'I can't believe she did this to you. But what about the boys? They're still at home.'

'Don't worry, Mum,' I said. 'Great-Aunt Maude looks after 'em like little princes. She's ever so fond of 'em. I think she likes babies. It's just me and Lily she doesn't like.'

We all felt better for a cup of tea, but there was no doubt that Mum was really worried. 'What do we do now?' she said and suddenly she covered her face with her hands as if it was all too much.

Mrs Stanbury was the kind of person who could find the answer to most problems. 'For a start,' she said, 'you've no need to worry. You can all come and stay at my house until you've sorted yourself out. Come on. I'll shut up shop early. We need to get these children something to eat.'

My knee was still painful, so Mum and Mrs Stanbury gripped my elbows to support me while I hobbled down the road as best I could. It probably took twice as long as it should.

By the time we'd reached Mrs Stanbury's house, Mr Stanbury was back from work at the cigarette factory. 'Why, if it isn't Daisy, our special papergirl,' he said. 'And who's this?'

Lily sniffed and wiped her tears on her sleeve. 'I'm Lily and I'm six.'

'And I'm Mr Stanbury,' he said, smiling.

'Are you a suffragette?' asked Lily. 'Daisy said the suffragettes will help us.'

'Well, I believe in the suffragettes' cause, Lily, and I'll certainly help you. But what happened? You both look as though you've been in the wars.'

'These girls have had to leave their home, Alfred,' Mrs Stanbury explained. 'I'm thinking that their father is likely to come looking for 'em so we should get them out of Bow as soon as we can.'

Mr Stanbury nodded. 'I agree. What are you thinking?'

Mrs Stanbury looked at Mum. 'I've been thinking that Edith Bryce might look after you. She lives with her grown-up son near the docks. Will that suit you?'

'If we'll be safe there, it will suit us fine,' said Mum. 'But are you sure she won't mind?'

'Absolutely not. Edith Bryce is a fellow suffragette. Her life's mission has been to help women like you.'

'I'm so grateful,' said Mum. 'I don't know how to thank you.'

'Not at all, lass. We're glad to help,' said Mr Stanbury

as he stood up and reached for his cap. 'I'll go round and tell Mrs Bryce what's happening.'

While he was away, Mum bathed my eye which was now so swollen I couldn't see out of it. At least my nose had stopped bleeding. That was a good thing. But my knee . . . ouch! It was so painful. Just touching it made me cry out.

'I don't think your leg's broken, Daisy,' Mum said. 'But you'll have to rest it for a while. Hopefully it'll soon be back to normal.'

Mrs Stanbury brewed more tea and made some fish-paste sandwiches, which were delicious. After that, Lily fell asleep on Mum's lap and I lay on the rug and dozed off for a bit.

When Mr Stanbury came back, he wasn't alone. It seemed to me that he'd brought a giant with him. He was so tall that he had to bend down to get through the door and his shoulders were almost as wide as two men. I felt scared of him at first, but that didn't last long.

'This is Mrs Bryce's son, Thomas,' said Mr Stanbury. 'As you can see, he's a big fella and nobody will bother you while he's around.'

They both laughed and I thought that Thomas looked kind in spite of his size. It turned out that he worked on the docks, just like Dad used to. So that accounted for the muscles on his arms. They were huge!

'Mr Stanbury says you've hurt your knee,' said Thomas kindly.

I nodded.

'Then I think I'd better give you a piggyback ride over to my house. Would you like that?'

I grinned. 'Oh, yes please!' I said. I hadn't had a piggyback ever since I'd grown too heavy for Dad to carry me. But I was sure Thomas would be plenty strong enough.

Lily looked disappointed.

'I like piggybacks too,' she said, blinking away a tear. 'My dad gives me piggybacks. He's ever so strong, he is.' Her head drooped and her bottom lip began to quiver.

Mr Stanbury couldn't resist her. 'Don't you worry, Lily. I'll carry you, love. Come on. Hop up.' And she looked up at him with a smile that would melt anybody's heart.

It must have been quite a sight to see us two girls riding piggyback and giggling all the way to the docks. We were going to a new home with Mum, well away from Great-Aunt Maude. Things were getting better. But in my heart I felt guilty leaving Dad and the twins behind, and I wished more than anything that they were coming with us.

Thirty-two

Mrs Bryce was waiting for us on the doorstep and she waved as we turned up Blair Street. There were houses on either side but it wasn't like Tuttle Street where we lived. Blair Street was wide with trees growing along it. Tuttle Street was narrow and dirty and always dark.

'Come in! Come in, my dears,' said Mrs Bryce, whose cheeks were as red and well-polished as apples. When we went into the front room a black-leaded grate was glowing with a coal fire, and the smell of new-baked bread was coming from the oven at the side of it. We hadn't always lived in two small rooms but even before Dad had his accident, the house we lived in wasn't as grand as this one. This one was bigger and warmer and very welcoming.

'This child's hurt her leg, Mother,' said Thomas as he gently lifted me off his shoulders. 'Pull out a chair for her, will you?'

There was a table in the middle of the room with four chairs round it – and I sat in one of them while Mrs Bryce knelt down to examine my knee. 'I think you'll have a nasty bruise in the morning, my love,' she said.

'But I don't think there's any serious harm done. So let me get you something to eat.'

The 'something to eat' was chicken soup and fresh bread warm from the oven. It was heavenly! And that was on top of Mrs Stanbury's fish-paste sandwiches we'd had earlier. We'd never eaten so much! But we were better for it. Even Mum's pale cheeks had turned a happy shade of pink.

Suddenly, Lily said, 'What about Dad? Shall we save some soup for him?'

I looked at Mum and she looked at me, hardly knowing what to say.

Eventually she said, 'Dad will be at home, Lily.'

'Won't he be looking for us?' she asked, her eyes wide as windows. 'He'll think we don't love him. But we only ran away from Great-Aunt Maude cos she was horrible to us.' Then she started to cry again.

'Lily's right,' said Mum. 'He'll be worried. We should let him know the children are safe at least.'

'You could send him a letter,' suggested Mrs Bryce.

'And I'll take it over, if you like. It's no trouble,' said Thomas.

'There wouldn't be any point,' I said, slightly embarrassed. 'Dad can't read very well.'

'Then I'll go and talk to him,' said Thomas.

But Mr Stanbury held up his hand. 'You can't go on your own, Thomas,' he said. 'He'll probably be upset. The man's lost his wife and children. And when men get upset, they can get angry. Two of us will be safer than one.'

'I can come with you,' said Lily.

Mrs Bryce swept her up into her arms. 'But I've got some chickens to feed, Lily,' she said. 'Would you and your sister like to help me?'

While Mum talked about grown-up things with the men, we went out of the back door and into a yard surrounded by a brick wall. Hens were strutting around making funny clucking noises and pecking at the ground while a cockerel with a bright red comb on his head gave a *COCK-A-DOODLE-DOO*. Lily was so excited that Mrs Bryce had to hold her hand to stop her chasing them.

'We've got six hens and there's the hen house,' Mrs Bryce said, pointing to a wooden shed. 'If you look inside, you can see Mabel. She's the oldest hen and she's sitting on her eggs, so we'll soon have some little chickens.'

'What's that over there?' I asked. There was a brick building in the corner of the yard, which Mrs Bryce said was a privy. Imagine! Your own privy! Not one you had to share with the rest of the street!

Mrs Bryce gave us some food for the hens. 'Now you sprinkle that on the ground,' she said.

Once Lily was let loose, she had such fun, skipping around, scattering the food and chasing the hens, which made them flap their wings and cluck louder than ever. I hadn't seen her so happy for ages.

My mind was on other things. 'Can I go to the privy?' I asked while Lily was running around. And Mrs Bryce said I could.

There was a gap at the top of the door so it wasn't really dark inside. Somebody had whitewashed the walls, which were very clean indeed. The privy itself was a piece of varnished wood with a hole in the middle, supported by bricks. It wasn't smelly like the privies I knew. In the alley at the back of our house in Tuttle Street, there was a row of four of 'em but only two had a door. They all stank something shocking.

I sat on Mrs Bryce's privy, looking around. There were a few cobwebs up in the corners but even the ceiling had been painted white. And, best of all, there were pieces of newspapers hanging from a nail on the wall. They'd been cut very neatly – each one about six inches square. Somebody had even threaded string through the paper. It was so clever. You just pulled off the top piece, wiped your bottom and then dropped it down the hole.

As if this wasn't exciting enough, when we went back into the house, I noticed that the room at the back had a tap in it with a big sort-of square pot underneath it, which Mrs Bryce said was a sink. She even showed me how to turn the tap on and water came gushing out like you've never seen!

'The water runs out down there,' she explained, pointing to a little hole in the sink. 'It goes down a pipe and into the privy and washes it clean. 'Isn't that a wonderful invention?'

I thought it was glorious! Water inside a house! I'd heard of such things but never seen it. How easy would it be to wash your hands and face *and* neck? I couldn't wait to tell Mum.

'You can have a bath tomorrow, if you like,' said Mrs Bryce, pointing to a large tin bath hanging outside the privy.

'Cor!' I said. 'That's big enough for two of us.'

'We'll heat up some water and we'll put the bath in front of the fire in the morning. Would you like that, Daisy?'

Oh yes, I would. It would be a dream, I thought.

Thirty-three

Mrs Bryce and Thomas didn't share the house with anybody else. They had the whole upstairs and the downstairs to themselves.

That night, Mrs Bryce took us up to the bedroom at the back of the house. 'I think you'll be comfortable here, for a while,' she said.

Well! What a beautiful room! There was a big bed and a washstand with a pretty china bowl and a jug of water so we could wash our faces.

The bed was lovely and soft with an eiderdown on top. We didn't sleep top to tail like we did at home. That night, we cuddled together – Lily on one side of Mum and me on the other.

Once Lily had fallen asleep, I whispered to Mum, 'I hope Thomas didn't mind giving up his bedroom.'

'It was very kind of him,' Mum whispered back to me. 'We must be sure to thank him tomorrow.'

By the time we woke up the next morning, Thomas had already left for the docks.

'Did he see Dad last night?' I asked Mrs Bryce as I sat at the table.

Before she replied, she turned away, attending to the

kettle on the fire so she didn't look at us. 'Yes, he did. Your dad said you were to be good girls and he'd see you soon.'

I noticed Mum looked nervous, and although she smiled and said, 'Of course you'll be good,' I thought she was trying to hide something.

'Are we going to school?' asked Lily.

Mum shook her head. 'I don't think so, darlin'. You'll be breaking up for the summer holiday next week, so you won't be missing much.'

I knew what she was thinking. Dad might slip out of the factory and meet us after school. Then he'd take us back home to Great-Aunt Maude. We wouldn't like that. But the law said we belonged to our father. That's what Dad had told us.

When we'd finished our breakfast, I limped into the kitchen, carrying the cups and plates. Mrs Bryce poured hot water from the kettle into the sink and she washed the pots while Mum dried.

Lily and me went to sit on the settee under the window and I thought this must have been where Thomas spent the night.

'This is a nice house, isn't it?' said Lily, bouncing up and down. 'I think Dad will like it here, don't you?'

Mum and Mrs Bryce were talking in the kitchen. 'I'm not sure I should go to Arber's today,' Mum said in a low voice so we wouldn't hear. But I had ears like a bat and I heard every word. 'I don't feel safe in Bow.

I'm afraid my husband might come looking for me or find out where I'm working. He'll be so angry about the girls. I don't know what he might do.'

'You stay here,' said Mrs Bryce. 'You look after Daisy and Lily. Mrs Stanbury will understand.'

Once they'd done the washing-up, I asked Mum if she'd look at my knee.

'It doesn't feel so good,' I said.

She knelt down and lifted my skirt. 'Oh heavens, Daisy. It's badly swollen and it's turned purple.'

When Mrs Bryce saw it, she clapped her hand over her mouth and said, 'Good gracious. It's looking worse. It must have swollen overnight.'

My knee was nearly as big as a football – really impressive! And I liked the thought of it turning purple. Mum and Mrs Bryce made such a fuss about it that I gave a groan every now and then to keep their attention.

'We should get you upstairs, my love,' Mrs Bryce insisted and I was helped back to bed with my leg propped up on a pillow.

Mum and Lily stayed with me all morning as if I was really poorly and Mum told me all my favourite stories, even the one about Florence Nightingale, because I was in pain every time I moved my leg. Mrs Bryce was ever so kind and brought me a beautiful green dress. 'When your knee's better, you can wear it, Daisy,' she said. 'My Elsie grew out of it long ago. You'll look lovely in it.'

'Does Elsie have any dresses for me?' asked Lily.

Mrs Bryce laughed. 'I'm sure she does but I'll have to look for one, Lily.'

That afternoon, Mrs Bryce left for a suffragettes' committee meeting in Bow. When she got back, she came up to see me right away and brought somebody with her.

'This is Doctor Murray and she's come to see you, Daisy,' she said as she walked into the bedroom. 'She was at the meeting and I told her about your accident.'

This was amazing. I'd never been treated by a doctor before. One came when Dad had his accident. But even when I had spots all over me, and a sore throat, and I thought I was going to die like my poor brother, Archie – even then *I* never had a doctor. And here I was, lying in a big bed all to myself with a doctor all to myself. *And* it was a lady doctor. I didn't even know there *were* lady doctors. So that was a surprise. She looked very smart in a navy-blue skirt, a crisp white blouse and a straw hat – like it was her Sunday best.

'Well now,' she said, smiling at me. 'Shall I take a look at your leg, Daisy?'

When she pulled up my skirt, she raised her eyebrows, surprised at what she saw. 'I can see your knee is swollen, but what are these bruises here?' By then, the marks left by Great-Aunt Maude's beating had turned red and were very clear.

'My great-aunt hit me with a wooden spoon,' I said. 'Then she threw her stick at me and I fell over. That's when I hurt my knee.'

The doctor nodded. 'Oh dear! You have been in the wars,' she said. 'Now let's see what we can do to make you feel better.'

She put her hand on the swollen part of my knee and I gave a shout just to show I was in pain. 'Hmm,' she said. 'That's rather hot. Can you bend it?'

I nodded and showed her that I could. 'It hurts, though,' I added, just to make sure she took it seriously.

Then the doctor said, 'Do you think you can stand up?'

So I shuffled off the bed. 'I can!' I said. 'But that hurts too.'

She watched me as I got back on to the bed and then she felt my leg and pressed it gently and I pretended to be brave but I groaned a bit.

'Well, Daisy,' she said, 'it's not broken. You're lucky. It's just a rather nasty sprain.'

'Are you going to strap it?' I asked. 'My dad was strapped up after he broke his leg at the docks. He had a splint too. Am I going to have one?'

She opened her bag and pulled out a roll of thick bandage.

'You won't need a splint,' she said. 'But I'll bandage your leg and you must stay off it for a few days. The swelling will have gone down by then.'

I was a bit disappointed about the splint but, as she closed her bag ready to leave, I said, 'Can I ask you a question, Doctor Murray?'

She smiled and said, 'Of course. What is it?'

'Was it hard getting to be a doctor? I thought only men could be doctors. Are you a real doctor?'

She pursed her lips together and held her head on one side as if she was thinking. 'Yes, I am a real doctor, Daisy,' she said as she perched on the edge of the bed. 'But when I was young, there were hardly any women doctors. Most people thought we weren't clever enough. And so I had to work very hard to prove that I was just as clever as any of the men.' She nodded her head. 'So to answer your question, Daisy: It wasn't *hard* to become a doctor – it was *very hard indeed*.'

I was amazed at her answer and I couldn't stop myself from asking more. 'Well, I want to be a nurse when I grow up,' I said. 'Do you think girls like me can go to that Florence Nightingale School? I really want to go there more than anything else. My teacher says I'm quite clever but Dad wants me to leave school and start earning money.'

Doctor Murray smiled. 'I can *see* you're clever, Daisy,' she said. 'But it's not easy for women. Many women are prevented from doing things that they are quite capable of doing. I sometimes think it's because men are afraid of how powerful women could be if they were only given a chance. That's why we've got to keep fighting for the vote so we can change things.' She stood up and brushed the creases from her skirt. 'I'll find out about the Florence Nightingale School and I'll let you know. I think you'd make a good nurse, Daisy. We need more girls like you.' And she walked out of the room.

Thirty-four

The first day in bed was brilliant. Everybody fussed over me – though I must admit I sometimes exaggerated a bit, and I made out that the pain in my knee was worse than it really was.

But on Saturday, I didn't have as much attention – which wasn't good.

'I've a lot to do, Daisy,' said Mum. 'I've promised to help make the banners for the suffragettes' procession in Victoria Park. Will you be all right up here by yourself? I'll only be downstairs and I can come to see you when I get a minute.'

'Where's Lily?' I asked.

'She's out in the yard with Mrs Bryce,' said Mum. 'The chicks are hatching and she's ever so excited. She's never seen chicks.'

I didn't like the idea of Lily having fun while I was stuck in the bedroom. That wasn't good at all.

Once Mum had gone downstairs, I slipped out of bed and looked through the window. There was no sign of Lily. She must have been inside the hen house watching the eggs hatch. I tried to imagine what the chicks would be like – fluffy little yellow things running about here and there. I'd seen some chicks once when I was little. I wished I could see them now.

I stood at the window for quite a while. I could see into the backyards of some of the houses opposite. There were two fat pigs with black spots in one of them. The pigs were grunting and turning up the soil with their snouts and making a real muddy mess.

In another one, an old lady was passing in and out of the smokehouse, getting the fire ready to smoke some herrings. The thought of those smoked herrings made my mouth water. I'd tasted them once, a long time ago. But now I could only go back to bed and dream about them.

The day after, I just couldn't bear being stuck upstairs a minute longer. I told Mum my leg was definitely feeling better.

'I can walk now, Mum. Honest!' I said. 'Let me show you.'

But she wouldn't listen.

'That leg is still swollen, my girl,' she said. 'You're to stay in bed until I say you can get up.'

Then Lily came upstairs after breakfast, holding something cupped in her hands.

'Look at this, Daisy,' she said. 'Mrs Bryce said I could show you.'

When she opened her hands I saw a tiny yellow chick, which jumped straight out on to the eiderdown and ran round and round, up and down, over my knees, chirping.

'What shall we call her?' asked Lily.

'Chicken Licken,' I said.

But Lily insisted on calling it Fluffy.

We laughed and laughed as we watched it scurrying about across the eiderdown. I bent my knee (the good one) and made a mountain for the chicken to climb – which it did without any trouble at all. I was sorry when Mrs Bryce popped her head round the door and asked Lily to take it back to its mother.

Not long after, I had a visitor. It was Mrs Bryce's sister, who was called Mrs Romano because she'd married an Italian man. She was just as friendly as Mrs Bryce and we chatted away for ages.

'I expect you're bored all by yourself, Daisy,' she said, sitting on the edge of the bed. 'So I've brought you some books. My children loved these, but they've grown up now so you can keep them if you like.'

One was *Alice's Adventures in Wonderland* and the other was *Treasure Island*. I was ever so thrilled. I'd never had a book of my own.

I was sorry when Mrs Romano left but, when she'd gone, I sat up in bed and read *Alice* all the way through. It was hilarious. I thought it was so funny that I went right back to the beginning and read it again. Much later, when it was time for Lily to come to bed, I told her the whole story and we looked at the pictures together.

'I like the white rabbit best,' she said. 'But I don't like the Queen of Hearts. She's horrible.'

Our new life away from Bow was working out just fine. Well, we all pretended it was anyway. I missed Dad and the twins and so did Lily because she told me so over and over. And I was sure Mum was upset even though she didn't say anything. Really, we all wanted to be back together. Poor as we were, being together was happier than being apart.

Thirty-five

On Monday, just to prove that I was absolutely perfectly better, I climbed out of bed and took the bandage off.

'Look, Mum,' I said. 'The swelling's gone down and it hardly hurts at all. I can go downstairs now. Honestly, I don't need to stay in bed any more.'

So Mum gave in and when I walked into the front room, Mrs Bryce was quite surprised to see me.

'Well, Daisy,' she said. 'That leg of yours has almost recovered. But maybe you should rest it for another day.'

That didn't sound good to me.

'I think Mrs Bryce is right, Daisy,' said Mum, picking up the banners they had been making. 'You should sit down and rest your leg for a bit longer. Just one more day.'

'I don't need to,' I said. 'What are you going to do? Can't I help?'

'Your mum's coming with me to the church hall,' said Mrs Bryce. 'She needs something to take her mind off those twin brothers of yours. I've told her I'm sure they're being well looked after – but mothers do worry, you know.'

Mum blushed and smiled, pretending she wasn't at

all worried. 'You could come with us, Daisy, but I don't think you should walk that far.'

'I can come with you, can't I, Mum?' Lily whined.

'If you promise to be good,' said Mum. 'We'll be making dresses.'

'Will I have a dress?' asked Lily.

'Well, they're really for the suffragettes' procession to Vicky Park. Miss Pankhurst brought some beautiful white fabric for us. But if there's some left over, maybe I'll be able to make one for you, Lily.' Then Mum turned to me. 'Do you know, Daisy, we've got special sewing machines. They're very modern. I'm really excited to be using them. I wish you could see them.'

'I wish I could, Mum,' I said, although cutting out fabric and making dresses sounded really boring. 'I think you're right. I should stay here and rest my knee,' I added. 'I don't mind. I've got my books to read.'

Reading would be good, I thought, and maybe I could slip into the backyard later and see the chickens. Or even go for a walk. That would be much better than watching people sew dresses.

Mrs Bryce made me some fish-paste sandwiches and put them on the table. 'There is one thing you could do for me, Daisy,' she said. 'Miss Emerson will be calling by this morning to pick up some handbills and a banner. If you're here, you could give them to her and then I won't have to wait in.'

Once they'd gone, I'd hardly started to read *Treasure*

Island when there was a knock at the door and I got up to open it.

A lady was standing outside on the pavement. 'Well, hello!' she said and I knew at once it was Miss Emerson. I remembered her from the meeting at Bow Baths Hall.

'I wasn't expecting to see a smart young lady. I've come to see Mrs Bryce,' she said in her funny accent. (At least I think that's what she said. But I couldn't be absolutely sure.)

'She ain't in,' I said. 'She's making dresses for the procession.'

'Oh, that's too bad,' she said as she breezed past me into the front room. 'But I see she's left me the handbills and the banner. Excellent!' She pushed them into a canvas bag and then she turned and smiled at me. 'I guess you'll have to introduce yourself, young lady. What's your name?'

Surprisingly, now that she was talking just to me, my ears soon got used to her accent.

'I'm Daisy,' I said. 'Mum and my little sister, Lily, have gone out with Mrs Bryce.'

'Daisy and Lily. Those are lovely names, I must say. Well, I'm pleased to meet you, Daisy,' she said, taking hold of my hand and shaking it vigorously. 'I'm a friend of Mrs Bryce. I'm Zelie Emerson.'

'I know,' I said. 'I saw you talk at Bow Baths Hall.'

'Ah, so you're a suffragette too,' she said.

'No, not really. I'm only . . . I'm only fourteen,' I lied.

168

(I was really only twelve!) I pulled myself up to my full height, making myself feel important. 'But I help Mrs Stanbury deliver the *Dreadnought* sometimes.'

She clasped my shoulders and laughed. 'That's just fantastic, Daisy. I help write the *Dreadnought*, you know! And fourteen's a great age to be a suffragette. What are you doing today?'

'Nothing,' I said. 'I'm just here by myself.'

'Wow! That doesn't sound like much fun. How would you like to come with me and give out some handbills?'

I didn't know what to say.

'Have you ever been in a motorcar?' she asked.

'A motorcar? No. Never.'

'Well, would you like to? You can come along if that's OK.'

'But what about Mum?' I asked. 'She'll wonder where I am.'

'Leave her a note on the table. But we won't be long. We'll probably be here before your mother gets back. Come on, Daisy, this is going to be an adventure!'

Thirty-six

When we stepped out into the street, there – right in front of my eyes – was one of those new-fangled motorcars. And this one was *huge*. I hadn't seen any like it in Bow and now I was going to ride in one. I couldn't believe it!

It was red with four enormous wheels and black leather seats – two in the front and two at the back. There was no roof or anything, so if it rained I knew we'd get wet. A man in a smart peaked cap was standing on the pavement, holding the door of the motorcar open ready for us to climb in. In the back seat, a lady (quite old) was sitting bolt upright, as stiff as a poker, wearing a posh hat with a veil over her face.

'Here we are, Griselda,' called Miss Emerson. 'I've picked up the handbills and I've brought a young friend along.'

The lady frowned and peered at me as if I'd wriggled out of a hole in the ground. 'Are we taking a child with us? Is that wise?'

Miss Emerson didn't answer. She turned to me and said, 'This is Lady Pointer,' and then she turned to the posh lady. 'May I introduce you to Daisy. She's fourteen and a fellow suffragette.'

The lady sniffed. 'She looks rather small for a person of fourteen years. She'd better sit in the front next to Morgan.'

Miss Emerson winked at me. 'You've got a great seat, Daisy. You're right next to the chauffeur.'

'What's a chauffeur?' I whispered.

'A man who drives a motorcar. You'll have the best view.'

She climbed into the back seat alongside Lady Pointer. Then Morgan the chauffeur opened the door at the front and said, 'In you get, miss.'

After that he walked round the front of the motorcar, bent over and turned a handle. He turned it once. Then twice. And the third time, as if by magic, there was a loud clanging noise as the engine started up. He climbed into the seat next to me and took hold of the wheel and we started moving. Oh, it was so good. We went much faster than a horse and cart and there was even a piece of glass in front of me and Morgan just to keep the wind off us. It was wonderful!

'We're working very hard, Lady Pointer, to win the votes for women,' Miss Emerson was shouting above the noise of the engine. 'I really hope that when you see what we do, you'll want to join us.'

'We shall see,' Lady Pointer shouted back. 'My husband is against the suffrage cause, as you know, but I'm interested to find out for myself.'

We travelled at such a speed that in no time at all we were in a grand part of London I'd never seen before. There were huge, beautiful buildings with lots of fancy glass windows and men in smart suits and bowler hats marching along the pavements.

Miss Emerson called to the chauffeur to stop the motorcar. 'Thank you, Morgan,' she said. 'We'll walk from here to the Monument.'

I'd never heard of the Monument but it wasn't far away and, when we got there, it was quite something. It was a tower built of stone with an entrance at the bottom and was so tall that it seemed to reach the sky.

'Why's it called the Monument?' I asked.

'It's a monument in memory of the Great Fire of London,' Miss Emerson told me. 'The fire was thought to have started near here. It's magnificent, isn't it? And there's a viewing platform at the top.'

'But how do you get up there?' I asked.

'Would you believe it,' she said, 'you have to climb up three hundred and eleven steps?'

Lady Pointer interrupted. 'That's all very interesting for this child but what has it to do with the suffragette movement?'

'I'm going to meet two friends here,' Miss Emerson explained patiently. 'At ten o'clock, they will climb to the top of the Monument and throw these handbills down and fly our banner,' she said. She smiled broadly. 'It should draw quite a crowd, I think.'

'Is that all?' asked Lady Pointer.

Miss Emerson raised her eyebrows. 'It's the modern way, Griselda. This is how we spread the word,' she said.

'We need people to know about our cause. We need the newspapers to take photographs and write about us. It's about deeds not words, these days.'

Just then, we saw a lady dressed in a grey coat and a straw hat waving her hand and hurrying towards us.

Miss Emerson smiled and waved back.

'Agatha,' she said, when her friend finally reached us. 'I'm so glad to see you – but where's Clara?'

'Oh dear, I'm so sorry but I think we'll have to call off our plans,' said Agatha. 'I'm afraid my sister's sick.'

'You don't look at all well yourself, if I might say,' said Miss Emerson. 'I appreciate you coming, Agatha, but I think you should go home and rest.'

And she was right. Agatha's face was as white as chalk.

They talked for a while and Agatha passed something to Miss Emerson, which she pushed under her coat. I noticed that Lady Pointer was frowning and pressing her lips together just like Great-Aunt Maude. She was definitely annoyed when Agatha walked away.

'It appears that our time has been wasted,' she snapped. 'Your suffragettes have let you down. I take it there will to be no demonstration now.'

Miss Emerson put her arm on my shoulder and gave me a wide smile. 'Oh, we suffragettes don't give up so easily,' she said. 'We've come all this way and I have the handbills and a banner – so Daisy and I will step into the breach. What do you say, Daisy?'

There was only one reply. 'Yes!'

Thirty-seven

'Are you sure, Daisy? Think you're up to it?' Miss Emerson whispered as we walked towards the Monument. 'You look fit and strong to me. Are you OK to climb those stairs?'

How could I say no? I didn't want to tell her about my bad knee because throwing handbills from the top of the Monument sounded unbelievably exciting.

'I can do it. We've got to show Lady Pointer, ain't we?' I said.

'Attagirl!' said Miss Emerson. 'She's a terribly influential woman. If we impress her today, she could really help our cause.'

As we walked towards the entrance of the Monument, Miss Emerson pulled some coins out of her pocket.

'Two tickets, please,' she said to the attendant, just as though we were ordinary visitors.

'You know how many steps there are, madam?' he said as he handed her the tickets.

'Oh yes, thank you,' said Miss Emerson. 'We'll take it steady. We're dying to see the view from up the top. I'm sure it'll be worth the climb.'

I counted every step and by the time we reached

one hundred and thirty-three, my knee was telling me it didn't like it. I was glad when Miss Emerson suggested we stop and have a little rest.

'I'm finding it tough, I must admit,' she gasped. 'I guess you'll be thinking I'm a real old woman, having to pause like this.'

I didn't tell her about my knee. I just said, 'Well, we need a break,' which is just what Mum would say. 'We can carry on when you get your breath back.'

We sat on the steps for a while and I began to feel a bit better. When we started to climb again we went slower than before – and with only one more rest we managed to reach the top.

There were two attendants waiting there.

'Well done, ladies,' said a bald-headed man with a large moustache.

We stood there for a few minutes, recovering from the climb. I was just waiting to see what Miss Emerson would do next.

'I expect you'll be wanting to take in the view from the gallery, ladies,' said the other attendant.

We smiled and nodded.

'Right then – just go through the door there and make sure you shut it behind you, ladies. It ain't half drafty in here when it's open.'

'Thank you so much, gentlemen,' Miss Emerson said as we walked out to the gallery, closing the door behind us.

'Those bars,' Miss Emerson whispered, pointing at two pieces of iron on the floor. She didn't say anything else. She just picked up one and I took the other. Quickly we slotted the bars into brackets on either side of the door. Once the bars were in place, the door was fixed tight.

My heart was already beating like the clappers, wondering what was going to happen next.

'The flag pole,' said Miss Emerson.

I gawped as she hauled down the city flag. Then I watched her pull something out from under her coat. It was the suffragettes' flag – purple, white and green – and she hoisted it to the top of the pole.

'That's brilliant, miss,' I said, staring at the flag as it flapped wildly in the wind. 'Everybody will be able to see that. Suffragette colours! You've done it!'

'We're not done yet, Daisy,' she said. 'Get the handbills and throw them over the side, will you? A few at a time. Make a real snowstorm of it.'

I grabbed the bag and took a handful before I leaned over the railings ready to throw them. But when I looked down . . . Oh crikey! My head began to spin and I felt sick. It was such a long way down that the people in the road looked like little black dots. 'Pull yourself together, girl,' I said to myself. With my eyes closed, I flung the handbills over the edge, sending them fluttering to the ground.

'Well done, Daisy,' Miss Emerson called. 'Keep going until you've got rid of every one of them.'

While I was scattering the handbills with my eyes shut, she was tying a banner to the railings. It was the one she'd brought from Mrs Bryce's house.

'What does it say?' I yelled against the wind.

'It says "Death or Victory" and it'll be seen for miles.'

This was the most exciting day of my life. 'We've done it, haven't we?' I said as I flung the last of the handbills over the edge. This time, I dared to look down and when I did, I couldn't believe my eyes.

'Look!' I called to Miss Emerson. 'People! There's a great crowd of 'em gathered round the Monument. Hundreds of 'em. They've come to see what's going on.'

Miss Emerson sank to the floor, laughing. 'Yes, we've done it, Daisy. We've done it. This is what I'd hoped for. It will be in all the papers.' She raised her hand and took hold of mine. 'Well done, Daisy. You're a real suffragette now. One hundred per cent suffragette.'

I was so thrilled by what had happened, I never wondered how we were going to get out of this sticky situation or what might happen next. I never gave it a thought.

Thirty-eight

What happened next was that the attendants tried to open the door.

'They must be wondering why we've been out here so long,' said Miss Emerson, shaking with laughter.

'Are you all right, ladies?' they called. 'The door seems to be stuck – but don't worry, we'll soon have it open for you.'

'We're just hunky-dory,' Miss Emerson called back, which made me laugh, especially as I didn't understand what 'hunky-dory' meant.

The attendants started banging on the door with something that sounded like a chair, but the door still didn't open so they gave up after a few minutes.

One of them called out to us, 'I'm sorry, ladies. It won't budge. But don't you go worrying your pretty little heads about it. My mate Freddy's going to get help and we'll soon have you out of there.'

We sat there, smiling and waiting patiently, knowing it would take ages to walk down all those steps. But even before Freddy had set off, we heard several pairs of boots – heavy boots – tramping up the stairs and someone shouted, 'Police! Stay where you are!'

Once they were at the top, they started yelling at the attendants.

'What were you thinking of? You've got two suffragettes out there flying their flag and flinging their handbills everywhere and we've got crowds of folk watching what they're up to. The press will be here before long, taking photographs.'

'We didn't know they was suffragettes, did we?' burbled one attendant. 'They just looked like ordinary ladies.'

'Well, of course they did. Or did you expect them to wear a sash that said, "I am a suffragette"?'

That made us giggle, I must say.

The policeman raged on and on. 'Why did you let 'em go on to the gallery by themselves, eh? Why weren't you watching 'em?'

'We don't always go with visitors,' said the attendant called Freddy. 'It's really windy out there.'

'Well, stand back, you stupid man,' said the policeman. 'Leave it to us. We'll soon get 'em sorted.'

While the bobbies were ramming their shoulders against the door, we leaned over the railings and started waving at the crowd below. I had a scarf Miss Emerson gave me and she had a large white handkerchief. There must have been hundreds of people gathered round the Monument and when they saw us, they started cheering as if they'd seen the King himself. Oh, it was such a good feeling!

The metal bars across didn't give way, no matter how many times those coppers bashed against the door. I think their shoulders must have been hurting really bad before they finally gave up.

'It's hopeless. It won't budge,' said one policeman. 'What we need is a twelve-pound sledgehammer. Walter! Run down and get one sharpish.'

'There's three hundred and eleven steps, gov! Why do I have to go?'

'Cos you're the youngest. Now stop arguing and get a move on.'

It took Walter ages to fetch the hammer and, in the meantime, the crowd had grown and grown. But when the sledgehammer finally arrived, it made short work of breaking down the door. Four red-faced policemen burst on to the gallery, pulled down the banner and quickly arrested us. I didn't resist or wriggle or complain. Like Miss Emerson, I stayed calm and dignified (even though my heart was pounding) and went back down the stairs following the policeman who led the way. There was much cheering from the crowd when we stepped out of the building and we smiled and waved to them as we were taken away to the nearest police station. I didn't like the thought of being locked up, but at the same time I was pleased to see so many people supporting the suffragettes. In Bow it felt like most people hated us.

'Name?' said a policeman behind the desk. He licked his pencil ready to fill in a form and stared at us.

Miss Emerson held her head high. 'My name is Mrs Shaw,' she said – which was a lie, of course. But I was glad I was with her. She'd been arrested before and was much calmer than me. She seemed to know what to do.

'And yours, miss?' he asked.

'Miss Spark,' I said, with my fingers crossed behind my back.

The policeman carefully wrote the names then slapped his pencil down on the desk.

'Right, lads,' he said to the four policemen. 'Put 'em in cells number two and three, will yer? We haven't had suffragettes in there. See how they like our hospitality.'

Well, their so-called hospitality was disgusting. I was pushed into a small dark cell with a plank of wood for a bed and a slop bucket for a chamber pot. Messages had been scratched on every surface and, worst of all, someone had smeared muck over the walls, which made me feel quite sick.

As the door of the cell was slammed shut and I was left alone, I suddenly felt more frightened than I'd ever felt before.

I sat on the plank of wood holding my head in my hands and began to tremble as I realised the consequences of what I'd done. Would I be sent to Holloway Prison like Miss Emerson and so many suffragettes? Would I have to go on hunger strike like Miss Pankhurst? Being a suffragette was a dangerous business, I realised.

I lay down on the plank to rest my leg, which was swollen again. Mum would be ever so cross if she knew I'd climbed up the Monument. And what if I was sent to Holloway Prison? What would Dad think if he found out? He'd never get over the shame of it. He'd never want to see me again.

In spite of these frightening thoughts, I must have fallen asleep, because I was woken by the noise of a key turning in the lock and the metal door swinging open with a clang.

I sat up and rubbed my eyes to see a policeman standing in the doorway. 'Right you are, miss,' he said. 'Come with me, if you please. You've got a visitor.'

I followed him down the corridor, wondering who it could be. Maybe it was Mum. But how would she know I was here? When we reached the front desk, there were two policemen with Miss Emerson. Nearby, standing tall and confident, was none other than Lady Pointer.

'I hope you haven't been treated badly, young lady,' she said, 'or I shall have something to say to the chief constable.'

She spoke with such authority that the policemen standing round the desk looked embarrassed, shuffling their feet and chewing their lips, as if they'd been caught swearing in front of the Queen. I almost felt sorry for them.

'I wasn't treated badly,' I said, 'but that cell was disgusting. It was filthy and really smelly.'

'Was it indeed?' said Lady Pointer, glaring at the policemen. 'Then I suggest you all get to work with a scrubbing brush and clean it up, instead of spending your time arresting innocent ladies.'

Then she turned away, holding Miss Emerson by the arm, and the three of us marched out with our heads held high and climbed into the motorcar, which was waiting outside.

'Home, Morgan!' Lady Pointer called to the chauffeur and we set off at a terrific speed, glad to be leaving the police station behind.

Thirty-nine

When Lady Pointer's car pulled up outside Mrs Bryce's house, I must admit my heart was in my mouth, wondering what I could say to Mum.

'Thank you for the ride, Lady Pointer,' I said ever so politely and waved as they drove away. I pushed my hand through the letter box, pulled out the string with the key on the end and unlocked the front door.

The house was empty. It was too good to be true. Nobody had missed me and Mum need never know I'd been dragged to a police station and flung in a cell. What a piece of luck!

I flopped on to a chair and put my swollen leg up on another one. Then I reached for the plate of fish-paste sandwiches and ate the lot (I was ravenous) before opening *Treasure Island*.

I hadn't read much by the time they all returned from the church hall. Lily came bursting in, followed by Mum and Mrs Bryce.

'Daisy! We had a lovely time,' she squealed, flinging her arms round me. 'Look! Mrs Bryce made this for my dolly.' Then out of her pocket she pulled a tiny white dress.

'That's nice,' I said. 'But you haven't got a dolly.'

'Mrs Bryce said there's one in a box upstairs. It used to belong to her daughter, Elsie, and she said I can have it now.'

I laughed. 'Then you're a very lucky girl.'

'It's a shame you couldn't come with us, Daisy,' said Mum, piling some white dresses on the table. 'I hope you weren't too bored.'

'No, I've been fine, Mum. I'm really enjoying *Treasure Island*.'

'Your mum's a wonder on that sewing machine,' said Mrs Bryce. 'She can make a dress in no time. Everybody was impressed.'

While she was piling more dresses on top of the others, I suddenly realised there was a problem. The note I'd left was still on the table. I should have thrown it away as soon as I got home. Why hadn't I? Now it was underneath the dresses. If Mrs Bryce read it, she'd want to know what I'd been up to. She'd be sure to read it to Mum and I knew she'd be furious.

'My knee's sore again, Mum,' I said, screwing up my face.

'Oh dear. Is it still bad?' she asked and she bent down to look.

This was my chance. I reached out and wriggled my fingers under the dresses on the table. But I couldn't feel the note. I couldn't reach far enough.

Mrs Bryce came hurrying over.

'That knee looks quite swollen again,' she said, shaking her head. 'You poor thing. It's just as well you rested today. I'll make you a nice cup of tea, eh?'

I nodded. 'And thanks for the sandwiches,' I said. 'They were delicious.'

'Glad you enjoyed them, dearie. Now let me light the fire so I can put the kettle on.' Then she looked at Mum. 'I think we'd better take these dresses upstairs before they get covered in coal dust.'

'Right,' said Mum. 'You stay there, Daisy. I might have to bandage that leg again. Keep it up on the chair till I get time to do it.'

She leaned over the table and picked up half of the dresses. Then she carried them up to the bedroom.

I held my breath as Mrs Bryce went to lift the rest of them. The note would be there for her to see. But as she gathered the dresses up, it was swept off the table.

'Oh, what's that?' asked Mrs Bryce as she watched it flutter to the floor.

'It's mine,' I said. 'I use it as a bookmark.'

'Lily, dear,' called Mrs Bryce, 'pick it up for Daisy, will you? My arms are full.'

But Lily was half way up the stairs following Mum.

'I can get it,' I said and I quickly hobbled across to pick up the paper and stuffed it into my pocket. My secret was still safe.

For the next week or so, everybody worked really hard making white dresses and designing more banners for the procession. Once the swelling in my knee had gone down, Mum agreed I could go to the church hall and help.

It turned out to be good fun – a bit of painting, some stitching and some extra-delicious sandwiches. But I kept wondering what would happen if Miss Emerson or Lady Pointer came in. What if they started talking about the incident at the Monument? The story of the great crowds and the police arrests was already in the newspapers. Then I remembered that the names of the suffragettes were given as Mrs Shaw and Miss Spark. So far, nobody knew it was Miss Emerson and me.

During that week, Mum was kept very busy and she seemed to be happy. Everybody praised her sewing and several ladies asked her if she would make dresses for them. But deep down I knew she was sad. Night-time was the worst. Quite often, when she thought that we were asleep, she would sob her heart out. I would snuggle up close to her, pretending to toss around in my sleep, and she would cling to me, her tears running down her cheek and on to mine.

I knew she was worrying about the twins. She must have been missing them something terrible. She was probably missing Dad too. And I bet he was missing her. They were childhood sweethearts from Ireland and they were happy together until all this suffragette business. We were a happy family. So why couldn't we be happy again?

Forty

By the next morning I'd made a decision.

I was going to talk to Dad. If I could make him see sense then everything would be all right. It wouldn't be easy. I knew that. But I was determined to be brave. After all, Miss Emerson had told me I was a real suffragette. 'One hundred per cent,' she'd said when I'd climbed up the Monument and thrown the handbills. That had been so exciting and now I felt it was time to carry on important work – getting my family back together again and making Dad understand that what we were doing was nothing to be ashamed of.

That day, we'd just finished eating Mrs Bryce's chicken and potato pie when I said, 'Could I go and see Eliza, Mum? I haven't seen her for weeks and I want to ask her to come to the procession on Sunday.'

Mum looked anxious. 'I don't know, Daisy. Should you go all that way?' she asked. 'It's quite a walk and it might not do that leg of yours any good.'

That wasn't really what she was worried about though. She was worried that I was going back to Bow and that I might go home. Poor Mum.

'I could walk with her,' said Thomas, who was not

long back from the docks. 'I'll see she's all right, Mrs O'Doyle.'

He was so kind, but the last thing I wanted was for him to come along and find out what I really planned to do.

'Oh, thank you,' I said. 'But I'll be OK.'

Mum raised her eyebrows in surprise. 'OK?' she said. 'Where did you get that word from, Daisy? It's not nice.'

Mrs Bryce laughed. 'Oh, Florrie, it's American. I've heard Miss Emerson say it many a time. Young people pick up things like that.'

Ooops! I should have been more careful. I didn't want them talking about Miss Emerson. Who knew where that might lead? So I stood up and said, 'I won't be long, I promise.'

'Can I come?' asked Lily. 'I like Eliza.'

Thank goodness Mum picked Lily up and said, 'Not today, pickle. You stay with me.'

It was quite a walk back to Bow and the nearer I got to Tuttle Street, the more nervous I became. When I turned the corner, three women were standing chatting on the cobbles. One was Mrs Pidgeon. She said, 'Hello, Daisy,' but the other two turned away which was quite rude. I was sure that even more gossip about our family would soon be spreading up and down the street. But good old Mrs Pidgeon came over to speak to me.

'Have you come to see your dad?' she asked.

'I have,' I said, knowing I could always be honest and straight with her.

'That's good,' she said. 'He's looking such a sorry soul these days. He had a cup of tea with me earlier. He told me he walks in the park a lot of an evening. Poor man. I think it broke him when you all left.'

I didn't like the sound of that and my stomach knotted. I felt really bad.

'So how's your mum?' Mrs Pidgeon asked. 'You're living with her, I'm guessing?'

I nodded. 'She misses the twins and she worries about them all the time,' I said. 'But I must get on, Mrs Pidgeon. I promised I wouldn't be back late.'

I ran up to number 34 and knocked on the door, quaking in my boots, waiting for Dad to come and not knowing what to say to him. But it was Great-Aunt Maude who opened the door.

'Oh, it's you,' she said. 'Well, you've got a nerve coming back here, and as for that mother of yours . . .'

'I want to speak to my dad,' I said.

'Oh, do you? Well, he's not here. He'll probably be at the Gunmaker's.' And she slammed the door in my face.

Tommy Watkins, Jacob Isaacs and the rest of the boys were now standing in a group further up the street, watching me. I didn't want to talk to them, but when I started walking away they came running after me.

'Hey, Daisy. Why've you come back?' It was Jacob Isaacs' voice.

I ignored him and hurried to the corner of the street. 'We thought you'd joined them crazy suffragettes,' he yelled after me. 'Have they kicked you out? Everybody round here hates 'em.'

Some of the lads laughed and said, 'Yeah, they do.'

Furious, I spun round to face them. 'And why do they hate suffragettes, eh?' I shouted.

They stood there, just a few feet away, shocked that I'd answered them back. Only Jacob Isaacs managed to think of something to say.

'Cos they do daft things and get put in prison.'

'They want things to change!' I called back. 'I suppose you don't want things to change, Jacob Isaacs.'

'No, I don't,' he said. 'Women belong in the house doing what their husbands tell 'em.'

'You mean, we should leave the running of the country to the men, do you?'

'Yeah!' he said. 'Men's brains are bigger than women's.'

'You've told me that before and it's still stupid.'

Then Tommy said, 'She's right! You are stupid, Jacob. She's a lot cleverer than you.'

Jacob turned and sneered at him. 'Oh yeah, Tommy Watkins. You're only saying that cos you're sweet on Daisy O'Doyle.'

Tommy flushed scarlet, raising his fists and I knew a fight was about to break out.

'Stop it!' I yelled at the top of my voice. 'Just listen to me.'

Tommy lowered his fists and they stood still, panting, waiting for me to speak.

'I'll tell you what the suffragettes are fighting for. What we should all be fighting for.'

Now I was really angry and I was going to tell them what I believed in. I was no longer a *secret* suffragette and I'd make sure they knew it.

'We want women to have a vote so we can change some of the unfair laws made by men,' I said. 'Mostly rich men in Parliament. We want everybody to have a good education and to put an end to poverty. If women get the vote, the politicians will have to listen to us – and we've got good ideas. We want change and won't stop fighting till we get it.'

I took a deep breath, wondering if I'd said too much. But Jacob just stood there, his mouth wide open, saying nothing. So I carried on.

'We believe in equal pay, equal rights and a chance to be what we want to be – not what you men think we should be. So that's what we're fighting for and I don't care whether you're behind us or not, Jacob Isaacs.'

There was silence and it seemed as though the whole street – boys and girls, women and men – had stopped what they were doing to listen to me. My heart was banging against my ribs and I was running out of breath. I thought I'd said enough so I decided to walk away.

That's when I turned round and saw Dad.

Forty-one

Together, we walked away from Tuttle Street with all those people staring at us. They weren't speaking. Just staring. Though I knew they'd be gossiping as soon as we turned the corner, and new stories about the O'Doyle family would go flying round Bow.

When we were clear of our street, Dad put his hand on my shoulder.

'It's good to have you back, Daisy,' he said. 'I must admit it was a real surprise to see you talking to them lads like that. But I was never more proud. Well done, my girl! That took guts, that did.'

I was so pleased when he said that, I broke into a smile, but I didn't know what to say. So I just said, 'Great-Aunt Maude told me you were at the Gunmaker's Arms.'

'She don't know everything, Daisy,' he said, squeezing my shoulder. 'Earlier Mrs Pidgeon called me in to have a cup of tea with her.'

'She's nice,' I said.

'Ah, she's a good old bird. She's the only one round here who doesn't tell me I'm a washout. She listens, does Mrs Pidgeon, and she's got a wise head on her shoulders.'

'So you didn't go to the Gunmaker's then?' I asked.

'I don't go there now. I don't have the money or the inclination. After I left Mrs Pidgeon I went walking round Vicky Park. I've taken to doing that of an evening,' he said. 'It's free. I've had to watch the pennies since your mum left.'

'She didn't leave, Dad,' I said. 'You kicked her out.'

'With good cause, my girl. With good cause.' And he dropped his hand from my shoulder.

There was a stubborn look on his face now. It wasn't a sunny face like it used to be – Dad telling jokes, Dad singing to us. I noticed he was thinner. Maybe he wasn't eating enough. Maybe deep down he was missing Mum.

We walked along for a minute in silence and at last he said, 'How's your mother?'

'She's upset, Dad,' I said. 'Ever so upset. She misses the twins something terrible.'

'I expect she does,' he said. 'Has she sent you to ask me if you can all come back?'

'She doesn't know I've come, Dad. But I'm sure she wants us to be together again. Like it used to be. And Lily and me want that too.'

Dad didn't speak for quite a while.

Finally he said, 'These last few weeks have been shaming for me, Daisy. The men at the factory mock me. They laugh at me behind my back. I know they do. I'm the man whose wife got mixed up with them suffragettes and got into trouble with the police. I'm the man who couldn't control his own missus and lost his kids. I'm weak. I'm a failure. That's what they say.'

'Dad,' I said, taking hold of his hand. 'Things have to change. Mum can't carry on with you telling her what to do all the time. Treating her like a slave, controlling her money. Mum should be able to make her own decisions and have some time of her own to go to suffragette meetings if she wants to. That's her right.'

Dad suddenly looked furious. His cheeks flushed and a vein in his neck pulsed angrily. 'So *you're* talking about rights now, are you? Well, I've got *my* rights, Daisy O'Doyle. For one thing, the law says that a man has the *right* to his children. That means, *by rights*, you and Lily should be living with me. I could send the bobbies round to fetch the two of you back.'

'No, Dad! You can't.'

'Oh yes, I can. That's the law.'

'And how will you find us when you don't know where we live?'

He reached for my arm and gripped it tight. 'Then you can come back with me right now. You can look after the boys and Great-Aunt Maude can go home to her own place. She's an old woman and she gets tired.' He looked me in the eye. 'You should be looking after them boys.'

I couldn't believe he'd said that. Hadn't he understood anything I'd told him?

I was angry all right, but I forced myself to calm

down. We were standing on the pavement and Dad was still holding on to me.

'I'm sorry, Dad,' I said. 'I know things are horrible for you but I can't stay with you. I don't want to. Not without Mum.' It was a hard thing to say but I had to. 'If you force me back home, I'll just run away again and I don't think you'd want that.'

I felt him loosen the grip on my arm. He closed his eyes and passed his hand over his forehead. My heart was breaking to see him look so unhappy.

'Just think about it, Dad,' I said quietly. 'Maybe you and Mum could meet and talk about how things could improve. That would be good, wouldn't it?'

'No, Daisy,' he said, shaking his head. 'Things don't get better for folks like us.'

'Don't give up. Help us to fight for things to get better.'

'I'm fighting just to feed the twins, Daisy. There's scarcely enough money for that.'

I put my hand on his arm. 'You should watch Great-Aunt Maude, Dad,' I said. 'She's been taking money out of the blue tin and she doesn't spend it on food.'

Dad's eyes widened and his mouth fell open.

'It's true,' I said. 'She spends it on beer when you're out.'

He didn't look angry. He looked defeated. His shoulders slumped and he slowly shook his head.

'I see,' he sighed. 'I'm glad you told me, Daisy. I'll

have a word with her when I get back. Now you get off to your mum.'

I know I hadn't got what I came for – a promise to talk to Mum – but I couldn't help flinging my arms round Dad's neck and clinging to him.

'One day soon,' I whispered in his ear, 'it'll all be right, Dad. Just you see.'

Forty-two

On Wednesday morning Mum said, 'It's not long until the procession and we need all the help we can get, Daisy. I'm sure we can find something for you to do.'

The procession was on Sunday afternoon. Hundreds of suffragettes would walk from the East India Dock all the way to Victoria Park, and they were going to be dressed in white and waving suffragette banners.

'Miss Pankhurst said we should all be nicely dressed, calm and well behaved,' Mum said, 'so that the police have no excuse to interfere.'

'That sounds like a good plan,' I said. 'We don't want to get bashed by the bobbies again, do we? Especially if Lily's there. How many dresses do you need, Mum?'

'We've made most of them already,' she replied, 'and some ladies have their own white dresses. So we only need another forty or so.'

Forty! Well, can you imagine how much cutting and measuring and sewing it takes to make forty dresses? I'd never made one in my life, but I said I'd do anything to help.

Lily burst into the front room, jumping up and down, holding the doll Mrs Bryce had given her. 'I'm going to take Peggy with me today,' she squealed. 'She's wearing her white dress, Mum. Look! She's beautiful, ain't she?'

We were all going to work in the church hall that morning and Mum persuaded Lily to leave the doll at home. 'After all,' she said, 'you don't want to get her dress dirty, do you, or she won't be allowed in the procession on Sunday.'

Lily looked very serious and held the doll close to her ear. 'Peggy says she don't want to go to no dusty old hall. She wants to stay at home and sit in Mrs Bryce's chair.'

So Mrs Bryce found a cushion, settled Peggy in the chair and kissed her goodbye.

When that was done, we all set off for the church hall where tables were set out with scissors, needles and thread. There were already ten or twelve ladies in the hall, cutting out the white fabric. Some of them had brought young children with them, and they were having fun running around the room. I noticed they were all dressed nicely and yet I could tell they weren't from posh families. They were just like us. It seemed to me that suffragettes passed on clothes to anybody who needed them.

At the far side of the hall, sewing machines were set on two tables. Mum went and sat at one and I followed her to find out what she was doing. I'd never seen a sewing machine up close before.

'It looks very complicated,' I said as I watched her put white thread through the machine needle.

'I worked on machines something like this at the shirt factory,' Mum explained.

The sewing machine was about eighteen inches wide – black with gold patterns on it. The word SINGER was written in gold letters across the middle. It was amazing! The needle was at one side and at the other was a wheel with a handle on it. Mum put some white cloth under the needle, then she took hold of the handle and turned the wheel.

'Wow, that's magic!' I said as the wheel made the needle bob up and down, pushing the fabric along and leaving a neat row of tiny stitches on the cloth. I couldn't believe how fast it was! So much faster than sewing by hand.

Soon, the room was crowded with ladies measuring suffragettes and cutting out patterns. Mrs Bryce beckoned me across to come and help her.

'It's the box of pins, Daisy,' she said. 'I'm afraid it was knocked off the table and the pins are scattered everywhere. Would you be a dear and pick them up?'

Picking up the pins meant crawling under the table and feeling around while trying not to get my fingers pricked. I was doing quite well until I heard:

'Hi, everybody! Gee, you all look busy!'

I recognised the voice of Zelie Emerson at once and my stomach began to churn. It wasn't that I didn't like her. No, I thought she was wonderful. But if she saw me she was sure to talk about our adventure at the

Monument. Everyone would hear and she'd tell Mum what a brave, daring daughter I was and – worst of all – how dreadful it was in those prison cells. It would be a nightmare. Mum would be so shocked at what I'd done. She mustn't find out. No, no, no! I'd have to stay under the table until Miss Emerson had gone.

But things didn't work out as I'd planned.

I'd been there for ten minutes or so when somebody shouted, 'Where's Daisy O'Doyle?' I stayed where I was, quiet as a mouse, my fingers crossed. Then Lily called out, 'She's under the table. I can see her over there.'

With a heavy heart, I crawled out and stood up as a lady in a blue dress and a cream straw hat came hurrying over.

'We need to measure you for a dress, dear,' she said and pulled out a measuring tape. Phew! I was in the clear. Well, that's what I thought, until Miss Emerson looked across the room and waved to me.

Forty-three

As luck would have it, Doctor Murray walked in just then and Miss Emerson was so busy talking to her, she probably forgot all about me. Once I'd been measured for a dress, I bobbed back under the table to carry on picking up pins.

I thought I'd picked up every single one and was wondering how long I could stay out of sight, when there was a murmuring round the church hall as if something exciting was happening. Then everybody stopped talking and the room went quiet. I poked my head out from under the table and saw that several ladies (including Miss Emerson and Doctor Murray) were standing near the door.

'Welcome to our suffragettes' sewing group,' somebody said. 'Please step inside and I'll show you round, Lady Pointer.'

Lady Pointer! I was horrified to hear that name. It was Lady Pointer who had taken us to the Monument in her car. She had rescued us from the police station. And now she was right here. I had to stay hidden. I had to!

After walking round the room meeting everybody, Lady Pointer decided to give a sort of speech.

'Thank you so much for inviting me here today. You are all working so hard for the cause of achieving the vote for women and improving their lives.' She cleared her throat and then she went on. 'I have some good news for you. My dear husband, Lord Pointer, has conceded that you have a worthy cause and he has agreed to help in any way he can.'

There was a sudden burst of cheers and it was some time before Lady Pointer started to speak again.

'You may be wondering why he changed his mind. Well, let me tell you. Last week, I saw for myself how determined you suffragettes can be – and how brave. This is what impressed my husband. I went with two of your own suffragettes into the heart of London where I saw them climb to the top of the Monument to send out the message of *Votes for Women* to the hundreds of people who gathered below. I also saw them ill-treated by the police.'

Whispers went round the room and I closed my eyes, covered my face and groaned. I knew what was coming.

'One of the suffragettes,' she continued, 'was none other than Miss Zelie Emerson.'

The church hall was filled with clapping and cheering as Miss Emerson stepped forward and said, 'Thank you Lady Pointer. It's true that I was one of those suffragettes but, most surprisingly, the young girl who helped me was only fourteen – and I tell you, she was so brave! She never complained, even when we were arrested and pushed into filthy cells at a police station.'

There were gasps all round.

'I know she's here today, so I'd like to thank her publicly. Where are you, Daisy O'Doyle?'

There was nothing for it but to come out of hiding to face everybody staring at me ... and clapping ... and cheering. They even laughed at Lily, who bounced around shouting, 'She's my sister! She's my sister!'

I didn't dare look at Mum. Luckily, I didn't have to because Doctor Murray came over.

'Daisy, my dear. Well done,' she said, shaking my hand. 'And now, I have some news for you. Remember you asked me to find about the School for Nurses?'

I nodded.

'Well, you'll be pleased to know that there's no reason why you can't train there.'

Oh goodness. That was wonderful news.

'You'll have to have an interview and probably some kind of entrance exam, but that shouldn't be a problem for a clever girl like you.'

Mmm! An exam. Maybe not such good news, I thought.

'Did you know that I run a surgery not far from the docks?' Dr Murray asked.

I shook my head.

'Anyone can come. Even if they can't afford to pay,' she said. 'I have two nurses working there and I was thinking you might like to come over and see what they do. They work very hard. Maybe, after a while, you could even help out. It would be very good experience for you.'

I could hardly stop myself from squealing like Lily. But I didn't. 'Oh yes,' I said. 'I'd like to do that ever so much, Doctor Murray. It would be the best thing in the whole world. Thank you. Thank you!'

'Good,' she said with a smile that spread right across her face like a sunbeam. 'Then let us say you'll come next Monday. There seems such a lot to do until the procession is over and I'm sure your mother will want you to help her. In the meantime, I've got a book you might like to read.' She pulled it out of her bag: *An Introduction to Nursing*.

'Oh, thank you, Doctor Murray,' I said and took it.

As she turned away to leave, she looked at me and winked. 'Quite a success at the Monument,' she said. 'Well done, Daisy!'

Forty-four

Mum wasn't half cross with me for going to the Monument. She said I shouldn't have gone with a stranger – let alone rode in one of them big motor vehicles. And I shouldn't have said I was fourteen when I was only twelve. And I ought to have told her where I'd been instead of keeping it a secret.

She was right of course but still, I didn't regret it. And I think deep down Mum was quite proud of me because I overheard her talking to Thomas about it that evening.

Anyway, the following morning we were all ready to go to the church hall (except Mum who was still putting on her hat), when Morgan, Lady Pointer's chauffeur, knocked on the door and handed me a letter addressed to Mum.

'What does it say, Daisy?' she asked.

While Morgan waited on the doorstep, I unfolded the piece of paper and read the letter out loud.

'Dear Mrs O'Doyle,

I am writing to ask you to visit me at my home this morning. I have something to discuss which I believe will be to your advantage.

Morgan will bring you and the girls in the car.

With kind regards,

Lady Griselda Pointer'

'Well I never!' said Mum, shaking her head. 'What does she mean? And why does she want to see *me*?'

'She's a good woman for all that she's well-off,' said Mrs Bryce. 'You go. You can come to the church hall after to do your sewing. Go on, Florrie! See what she's got to say.'

Morgan was still waiting. 'You've only got to step into the motorcar, missus,' he said. I expect he was getting bored just standing there.

Mum looked really flustered. 'I don't know nothing about motorcars,' she said.

I tugged her sleeve. 'You don't need to know anythin', Mum,' I said. 'Go on. I'll sit in the front and you climb in the back with Lily.'

'Just what I was going to suggest,' said Morgan, and he opened the door at the back of the car and gave a sort-of bow which made Mum blush as she climbed in.

I was used to the speed of the motorcar, of course, but Mum wasn't and she squealed every time we went round a corner and had to cling on to her hat to stop it blowing away. Lily, however, laughed and giggled all the way and enjoyed the ride so much, she was sorry when it ended.

Eventually the motorcar turned up a long tree-lined drive, which led to a big house. Oh, it was a marvel – with lots of tall windows and pink roses growing up the walls. Fancy me knowing somebody who lived in a house like that!

Morgan pulled up outside the front door, which was opened by a maid in a smart black dress with a spotless white apron over the top.

'Good morning, Mrs O'Doyle,' she said as we climbed out of the motorcar. 'Lady Pointer is waiting for you and your daughters in the drawing room. Please come this way.'

She led us across a massive hall with black and white tiles on the floor. Then on through double doors. A large brown dog with a shaggy coat came galloping towards us, wagging its tail like mad.

'Here, Bruno,' called Lady Pointer, standing up from a gold velvet armchair. But the dog didn't take any notice. He just seemed glad to see us.

'Come along in, all of you,' Lady Pointer said. Then she waved her hand towards a large leather settee in front of the fire. 'Please, sit down.'

So we all perched on the edge, feeling very nervous on account of never having been in such a grand house before. The dog sat by us, leaning against my legs and occasionally turning to lick Lily's hand. I was amazed he was allowed into that grand room with its beautiful carpets and fine furniture. I was overwhelmed by it all. I think Mum was too. But Lily was too busy stroking the dog to notice much.

Lady Pointer looked up at the maid. 'Thank you, Annie,' she said. 'Bring the tea now, if you please.'

And before we knew it, a tray appeared with four

china cups and saucers, a silver teapot, a small jug of milk and a little bowl of white sugar cubes.

'I expect you're wondering why I asked you here,' Lady Pointer said to Mum as she poured some milk into each cup.

'Yes, I am, m'lady,' Mum replied ever so politely.

'Well, I've been very fortunate in my life, my dear, and I like to help out where I can.' Then she picked up the silver teapot and poured the tea. 'Mrs Bryce is a splendid woman and she has told me of your difficult situation. So this is how I should like to help you.'

It turned out that her husband, Lord Pointer, owned several houses in Mosswood Street, not far from where Mrs Bryce and Thomas lived.

'One of the houses is unoccupied,' said Lady Pointer, 'and my husband would be happy to let you and your daughters live there free of any charge until you can afford to pay the rent – or until you return to Bow.'

'But I couldn't poss—' Mum stuttered.

'Let me finish, my dear. I have seen the dresses you have made and you are obviously very talented. If I provide you with a sewing machine, I believe you could make a good living making dresses.' Mum tried to interrupt again, but Lady Pointer held up her hand. 'To start with, I should like you to make something for me. I have a roll of beautiful blue silk my husband brought back from India. It would be a splendid dress, if you would agree to make it.'

Mum sank back on the settee looking stunned, as if she couldn't take it all in. Lily was busy eating the sugar cubes and playing with Bruno. So it was up to me to speak.

'That sounds wonderful, Lady Pointer,' I said. 'I think you're right – Mum would make a really good dressmaker.'

'Indeed,' said Lady Pointer. 'Well, that's settled then. Doctor Murray has told me that you hope to be a nurse one day, young lady.'

'Yes I do,' I said. 'And she's going to help me. She said I could go to her surgery and watch the nurses and learn from them. Oh, I can't wait.'

Lady Pointer beamed. 'You're a smart girl, Daisy. I'm sure you'll succeed.' Then she looked at Mum. 'You have a clever daughter, Mrs O'Doyle. I congratulate you.'

Mum sat up, smiled at me and nodded. 'Oh yes. She's a clever one all right.'

Forty-five

Well, I can't tell you how exciting it was. We actually moved into the house that evening. Mrs Bryce and Thomas walked round with us to number 10 Mosswood Street (that was our new address) and we couldn't believe what a lovely house it was. There were two bedrooms. The one for me and Lily was at the back and had two beds in it.

'Can't I sleep with Daisy no more?' Lily complained. 'It won't be nice all by myself.'

So we pushed the beds close together. 'Will that do, Lily?' I asked, and she seemed happy enough.

The other bedroom had a big bed.

'Is that for you and Dad?' Lily asked but Mum didn't answer.

'Let's go downstairs,' she said.

Mrs Bryce and Thomas were in the backyard.

'You'll have plenty of room for chickens here,' Thomas said as we walked outside. 'You can have some of ours, if you like, when the next lot are hatched.'

Lily started squealing and jumping about. 'Oh yes. Can we, Mum? Can we have chickens? I'll look after them, I promise. Can we?'

Poor Mum tried to calm her down by saying, 'We'll see, Lily.'

Our new house was very like the Bryces'. There was a privy in the yard and a water tap and a sink in the back kitchen. As for the front room, well . . .

There was proper furniture – a square table with four chairs, a horsehair sofa under the window *and* a sideboard. I couldn't believe it! Even the cupboards were filled with plates and cups and things.

'Look at that grate, Mum,' I said. 'It's got an oven to cook in. You'll be able to bake bread like Mrs Bryce!'

'And there's plenty of coal in the scuttle,' said Thomas. 'You'll be able to have a nice fire.'

I think Mum was overwhelmed by it all. 'I never expected anything as grand as this,' she said, brushing a tear from her eye as we stood together in the front room. 'Everyone's been so kind.'

And then – as if that wasn't enough excitement for one day – somebody knocked at the door. When we opened it, there was Morgan.

'Lady Pointer would like to know if Mrs O'Doyle finds the house satisfactory,' he said.

'Oh yes, indeed it is,' said Mum. 'More than satisfactory. Everything is marvellous. Thank you, Mr Morgan.'

The chauffeur nodded and turned to the motorcar, which was right outside our front door. He picked up a wicker basket from the back seat, carried it into the house and set it on the table. Then he went back to the car and we all watched in amazement as he lifted out a wooden box and a brown-paper parcel.

'With compliments of Her Ladyship,' he said, smiling, as he put them on the table next to the wicker basket.

'Thank you, Mr Morgan,' said Mum. 'I don't know what to say. Lady Pointer is very generous. Please thank her for me.'

And with a bright smile and a wink my way, he left.

We couldn't wait for Mum to open the basket. We just knew there'd be something grand inside. And there was! It was packed with bread, butter, cheese, pickles, fish paste, apples, potatoes, carrots, onions and a rabbit.

'You'll have a feast!' said Mrs Bryce, clapping her hands in delight. 'That rabbit will make a grand stew.'

Lily begged for an apple and Mum cut one in half for the two of us and it tasted like heaven. Honest! We munched away while Mum took the lid off the wooden box.

'Oh my goodness,' she said, clapping her hands to her cheeks. She was bowled over by what she saw. 'This is too kind.'

Inside the box was a sewing machine. It was beautiful – black and decorated with gold patterns.

'My very own machine,' she said. 'How can I be so lucky?'

'What about that parcel, Mum?' asked Lily, her mouth full of apple.

Mum's fingers were shaking as she untied the string that was wrapped round it. And when she smoothed back the brown paper, we saw some lovely blue fabric. I'd never seen anything like it. It was smooth and shimmery like butterfly wings.

'It's Lady Pointer's silk from India,' said Mum, her voice choking as she spoke. 'She's asked me to make a dress for her,' she explained to Thomas. 'It's the most beautiful fabric I've ever seen.'

Mum had had a hard life and she couldn't believe she had found so much kindness. It was all too much for her and she burst into tears. Mrs Bryce put her arms round her and Mum sobbed and sobbed.

I think Thomas was a bit embarrassed seeing Mum cry, so he went out into the backyard and lit his pipe. Lily and I went with him and asked about chickens and how we should look after 'em. We learned quite a lot so I felt sure we'd be able to manage them when they arrived.

'We should have lots of eggs,' I said.

'But we'll have to have names for the chicks,' said Lily. 'What will you call yours, Daisy?'

I shrugged. 'That depends what they look like, Lily,' I said. 'You can't go thinking up names for brown hens when they might be black and white. We'll have to wait and see, won't we?'

When we went into the house, Mum was back to normal except for a red nose. But she did look happy.

On Friday morning Mum went and took Lady Pointer's measurements so she could start making the blue silk dress. Apart from that we went down to the church hall to help finish the white dresses and the banners. Once I was allowed to sew letters on to a banner but I wasn't very good and the words looked rather wobbly and had to be unpicked. That was the last time I did any sewing. Instead, I was sent to give out handbills so that everyone would know about the procession to Victoria Park on Sunday. That was much more fun.

The night before the procession, we were all very excited.

'Would you like to sleep in my bed tonight?' Mum asked and we shouted, 'Yeah! Let's all sleep together!'

So we all snuggled up and felt warm and happy. I think being in that big bed by herself made Mum feel sad. She must have missed Dad and the twins ever such a lot.

That's what I thought anyway.

Forty-six

We woke up on Sunday to a lovely sunny morning. We couldn't wait to put on our white dresses, which were shorter than normal dresses and looked ever so modern. Miss Pankhurst had said they should be four inches shorter so they didn't trail in the mud if it rained – which I thought was very sensible.

The dresses weren't the only thing. We had straw hats too, and Mrs Bryce had decorated them with paper flowers. Mum had a really beautiful one that Miss Emerson had given her.

'You take it,' she'd said one day at the church hall. 'I've got too many hats, anyway. And it looks so much better on you, Mrs O'Doyle.'

I wish you could have seen Mum. She looked ever so pretty all in white with her suffragette sash – purple, white and green – over her shoulder.

I wished Dad could have seen her too. But I don't suppose he'd have been pleased to know she'd be marching with the suffragettes. I wondered where he was and what he was doing that Sunday. I couldn't help wishing he was going with us.

'Do I look nice, Daisy?' Lily asked, standing in the front room clutching her doll.

'You look beautiful,' I said. 'And Peggy looks very smart in her white dress. Two proper little suffragettes!'

She giggled and hugged the doll tight as Mrs Bryce opened the front door.

The procession was starting from the gates of the East India Dock. By the time we'd walked there, other people had already arrived, as well as a brass band in their dark blue uniforms with gold braid. When we set off, the band was at the front playing loud marching tunes and we walked behind carrying banners and waving flags. Thomas and one or two other men helped carry the banners, which were quite heavy, with wooden poles at each end.

One said 'Votes for Women' and another said 'Deeds Not Words'. But my favourite was:

'Through Thick and Thin

We Never Give In.'

I must admit, I was disappointed that there were only about fifty of us marching to the park. I didn't think this was a good show. I'd expected more.

'Don't you worry, Daisy,' said Mrs Bryce. 'There'll be plenty joining us along the way.'

'What will it be like when we get there?' I asked.

'You'll meet lots of suffragettes,' she said, 'and there'll be speakers standing on platforms – or maybe they'll be on the back of a cart! But it's going to be peaceful. That's the aim today.'

I couldn't imagine a suffragette standing on a cart. 'Will Miss Pankhurst be there?'

'Probably not. She's still not well. But Miss Emerson will be speaking.'

'She talks funny,' Lily said.

'But she's very nice,' I added.

'There's a suffragette who comes from Australia. She's called Muriel Matters. She might be there,' said Mrs Bryce.

'Does she talk like Miss Emerson?' I asked.

'No, not really. She has an Australian accent,' said Mrs Bryce. 'She travels around the country in a little horse-drawn caravan telling people all about the suffragette cause. She's very brave. In one village they threw bad eggs and rotten fish at her.'

'That's horrible,' said Lily. 'And very rude!'

'But she didn't give up,' Mrs Bryce went on. 'Once she chained herself to a grille inside the House of Commons and shouted "Votes for Women" until the police came and cut the chains.'

'I suppose they arrested her,' I said.

Mrs Bryce nodded. 'They sent her to Holloway. But when she came out – you know what she did?'

'No.'

'She hired a hot air balloon with "Votes for Women" on the side. It floated up high towards the Houses of

Parliament with Miss Matters riding in the basket hanging under the gasbag. She was hoping to scatter handbills over the King as he walked to Parliament.'

'Blimey!' I said. 'The King must have been angry.'

'No. Unfortunately, the wind was very strong and blew the balloon off course. So she never got there.'

Lily and I started to giggle. Mrs Bryce was such a good storyteller I hadn't noticed that more and more women (and some men) had joined us as we walked along.

'Look! There's Mr and Mrs Stanbury on the pavement,' I said. And they came rushing over, as pleased as punch to see us. They walked with us the rest of the way, chatting and exchanging the latest news, and we told them all about our new house and my adventure with Miss Emerson.

By then there were hundreds in the procession, blocking the roads on the way to Victoria Park. Everybody was waving flags and singing. There were special suffragette songs – but this was the one I liked best:

Shout, shout, up with your song!
Cry with the wind for the dawn is breaking.
March, march, swing you along,
Wide blows our banner and hope is breaking.

It was as if we were going to the biggest party ever.

Forty-seven

By the time we reached Victoria Park, we were pressed close together as more people joined with the procession and tried to push their way through the gate.

Lily clutched my hand and said, 'I don't like it, Daisy.'

But suddenly we were through and a woman wearing a sash reading CHIEF MARSHAL called, 'Move along to Platform One for the opening ceremony. Quick as you can, please. There are hundreds of people behind you waiting to get in.'

Once we were through the gate, everyone rushed forward towards the far end of the park, where a platform had been set up on the grass with a huge number one at the side.

'Stay close, Daisy,' said Mum. 'Everybody will want to see the opening ceremony and I don't want to lose the two of you.'

Quite a crowd had already gathered in front of Platform One and more were following behind us. Soon we were squeezed like sardines in a tin and Mum had to pick Lily up because she was crying.

All of a sudden, a bugle sounded and the noisy crowd quietened down. I stood up on my toes to get a better view as a woman climbed unsteadily on to the platform. Like the rest of us, she was wearing a white dress and a large straw hat decorated with flowers. But I could see she was thin and pale.

'It's Miss Pankhurst,' I gasped. 'I'm sure it is.'

'Good heavens!' said Mrs Bryce. 'How has she managed to get here?'

People around us said, 'Shhhh!' so we kept quiet after that.

'I am honoured to open this important meeting in support of the suffragettes' cause,' Miss Pankhurst said. 'I am proud to see so many of you here today. We are still fighting for the simple right of women to vote and to take their place alongside men.' She stopped and looked as if she might faint. But she took a breath and somehow carried on. 'We must keep on fighting,' she gasped. 'Thank you all. I hope you enjoy your afternoon.'

The crowd roared. Miss Pankhurst raised her hand, smiled and stumbled off the platform.

'Sylvia Pankhurst is as brave as her mother,' said Mrs Bryce, wiping a tear from her eye. 'But she's not well enough to stand up and talk in front of a crowd. She should be in bed.'

The opening ceremony was over and everybody drifted away from Platform One. By then, the sun was high in the sky and Lily and I were hot so we ran over to a drinking fountain and quenched our thirst before joining Mum. She had found a nice shady spot under a tree and was sitting on the grass with Mrs Bryce and Thomas.

'Would you girls like a bun?' Mrs Bryce asked.

'Oh yes, please,' said Lily and Mrs Bryce reached for a bag and pulled out some current buns. She must have baked them early that morning specially. That was just like Mrs Bryce. Always thinking about other people.

'We're having a picnic, ain't we, Mum?' said Lily.

'We are,' said Mum. 'And I've brought some egg sandwiches so we can have another picnic later.'

'Can't we eat them now?' Lily asked. But Mum said no.

We could see four platforms from where we were sitting. On three of them, suffragettes were talking to the crowd. On the fourth one, there was a man.

'That's Mr Lansbury,' said Thomas, pointing to the platform in the distance.

'I've never heard of him,' I said. 'Who is he?'

'He was our Member of Parliament not long ago,' said Mrs Bryce. 'He's lived round here for years and he works hard for women's rights.'

'He was sent to prison and he went on hunger strike,' said Thomas, getting to his feet and brushing crumbs off his suit. 'He's a good man. I wish there were more like him. Anyway, I'm going to see what he has to say. I'll see you later.'

'If we lose each other,' Mrs Bryce called after him, 'we'll meet up at the bandstand at three o'clock, shall we?'

'Right you are, Mother. See you later,' he replied and walked away.

'Do we have to watch people talking, Mum?' asked Lily. 'I don't like it. I thought this was going to be a party.'

Of course she didn't like that kind of thing. She was only six. It must have seemed really boring to her.

'I'll take Lily over to the lake, shall I?' I said but Mum shook her head.

'It's too busy in the park today, Daisy. I don't want you two getting lost. I'll come with you.' She stood up and took hold of Lily's hand. 'You can paddle at the edge of the lake, Lily, as long as you don't get your dress wet.'

Then Mrs Bryce said she'd come with us too, to keep Mum company.

Although the park was huge, that day it was crowded with people walking around carrying banners and waving flags and generally enjoying themselves. There were pathways criss-crossing from one side of the park to the other and one or two people were driving along in open-top carriages. There was one with three children in the back holding a banner that read 'Deeds Not Words'. It was pulled by a black and white pony – really nice! Later we saw another carriage with two old ladies in it. They were wearing suffragette sashes across their chests. When they saw us staring, they laughed and waved and called, 'Votes for Women.' So we shouted the same.

'I don't expect those ladies can walk very far,' Mrs

Bryce said to Mum. 'I wouldn't mind having a ride in a carriage, would you? My feet could do with a rest.'

It was quite a walk to the lake but it was worth it. Lily and I took our boots off and left Mum and Mrs Bryce sitting on the grass. We ran down to the edge of the water and dipped our feet in. Our toes were hot after all that walking and the water was cold. It felt perfect.

'Lift your dress up a bit, Lily,' I said, 'or it'll get wet.'

But she just grinned and ran away, expecting me to chase her – which I did. Round and round. Up and down. Giggling and laughing until we were too hot to run any more. We had such fun that afternoon – but before we knew it, Mum was calling us to come out of the water.

Lily didn't want to. 'Can't we stay?' she asked.

'Don't make a fuss, Lily,' said Mum. 'You've been in there for a long time and you've had your fun. Come and dry your feet on the grass. We're going back to hear Miss Emerson speak on Platform Three.'

Lily pulled a face.

'You know Miss Emerson,' I said. 'She's that nice lady with the funny accent. She needs us to cheer her on.'

As we crossed the park, the sun was still beating down. We were tired by then and our steps were slow. All except Lily, who was skipping ahead, swinging Peggy in her hand.

She was quite a way from us when she suddenly stopped and squealed. It was a squeal of excitement – like when somebody gives you a parcel and, when you open it, there's something inside that you never thought you'd have in a thousand years. It was that kind of squeal.

Then she shouted, 'Dad! Dad!' and ran at full pelt with her arms outstretched towards him on the other side of the pathway.

There was no stopping her. Even though Mum and I shouted, 'No, Lily!' she went on, her eyes fixed on Dad. She didn't see the carriage coming but the horse saw Lily. He reared, his hooves rising high in the air, paddling frantically and trying to avoid her. But he couldn't hold them back for long and with a terrifying whinny, his hooves came crashing down on my little sister.

Forty-eight

So many things happened. I can't remember all of it.

But I remember Dad dashing over to Lily and Mum doing the same. And Mrs Bryce.

I remember picking up Lily's doll, her dress dirty and badly torn.

I remember the two ladies climbing down from the carriage and rushing over, horrified by what had happened and trying to help. The third lady, who was the driver, was tugging the horse's reins and pulling him away, trying to calm him down.

I remember Dad kneeling down, wrapping his arms round Lily and saying her name over and over. But she lay there, her cheeks as white as paper.

'Oh heavens! There's blood on her head, Patrick,' sobbed Mum. 'Look, there in her hair. We've got to get a doctor.'

'First get her home,' said Mrs Bryce. 'She needs looking after.'

Mum turned to Dad. 'She'd better come to my house, Patrick,' she said. 'There's a comfortable bed there.'

Dad nodded as if he knew that Tuttle Street was not

a good place for a sick girl. 'Will I come?' he asked. 'Will that be all right? I must be with her, Florrie.'

'Of course,' Mum whispered. 'Of course you must.'

One of the ladies said, 'We can take you home. You can both sit in the back of the carriage with your daughter.'

But the horse was still skittish. 'I'm sorry,' the driver called. 'I can't calm him down. He's too frisky.'

The other lady said, 'Oh dear. That's dangerous. We don't want another accident, do we? Can you carry the little girl up to the road, do you think? You'll be able to get a motor cab to take you home.'

A third lady opened her purse and pushed some money into Mum's hand. 'Take this to pay the cabbie,' she said. 'And here is my card with my address on it. Please let me know how your little girl recovers. We shall be thinking of you.'

Dad stood up, lifting Lily so gently she must have felt cushioned in his arms. He walked across the grass towards the gate, carrying her as if she were no heavier than a bundle of feathers.

But Lily didn't move or open her eyes. She flopped as lifeless as her doll.

Mrs Bryce said, 'I'm going to run ahead of you and get a motor cab. At least it'll be quicker than the old horse-drawn ones.'

'I'll come with you,' I said. 'Two's better than one.'

People were already leaving the park and when we

got to the road, some were waiting on the pavement for a motor cab to take them home.

'We've got an injured child coming through,' Mrs Bryce explained. 'Her father's carrying her. Could we go in the next cab that comes? We need to get her home as quickly as possible.'

A group quickly gathered round Mrs Bryce, wanting to know what had happened. But before she had told them the whole story, I saw Mum and Dad.

'They're here,' I shouted. 'They're coming through the gate.'

Just as they arrived, a motor cab came round the corner and a man in the crowd flagged it down.

'You take this one,' he called to Dad. 'Get the child home. And good luck to yer.'

The driver jumped out of the cab and helped Dad put Lily on the back seat, her head on Dad's lap and her feet on Mum's knee.

'You sit in the front, Daisy,' said Mrs Bryce. 'I'm going to look for Doctor Murray. I think I know where she might be. We'll come over to Mosswood Street as soon as we can.'

The cab set off, whizzing along at such a speed I thought Mum might be scared. But she didn't scream or anything. I think she was just concentrating on Lily. When we were almost home she suddenly said, 'Patrick! Lily's eyes flickered just then! I'm sure they did.' And I quickly looked over my shoulder to see for myself.

All I could see was Dad staring at Lily as if he was trying to see some movement.

Then he shook his head sadly. 'I don't think it was anything, Florrie,' he said. 'Try not to worry yourself. I think our girl will be as right as rain after a good sleep.'

The driver of the motor cab was very kind. He wouldn't take any money. 'Glad to be of service, governor,' he said to Dad. 'I hope all goes well for yer.' And he drove off.

Mum led Dad up the stairs and into her bedroom and I saw Dad glance at the blue silk dress that Mum was making for Lady Pointer. It was hanging in the corner.

Dad laid Lily gently on the eiderdown. Mum looked at her lying there, still not moving, and tears rolled down her cheeks.

'She feels cold,' said Dad, and Mum ran into our room, fetched a blanket and covered her with it.

We all stood round the bed, saying nothing, our eyes fixed on Lily. We must have been praying for the same thing – 'Please open your eyes, Lily. Please let us see you smile again.'

After half an hour there was a knock at the front door and Mrs Bryce and Thomas came rushing inside. 'We're here, Florrie,' Mrs Bryce called, 'and we've brought the doctor.'

Mum ran to the top of the stairs. 'Oh, thank goodness. Come straight up, Doctor Murray. I'm so sorry to bother you but she still isn't moving.'

Dad seemed surprised when the doctor walked into the bedroom. I think he was expecting a man.

'Mrs Bryce has told me what happened to Lily,' said Doctor Murray, shedding her jacket and putting her medical bag on the floor. 'I'm so sorry. But let me take a look at her.'

We all stepped back from the bed to give the doctor some space. We watched her open Lily's dress and look at her chest. Then she leaned over, putting her ear to Lily's mouth, listening for breathing. But she said nothing. She took hold of Lily's wrist next. 'I'm feeling for her pulse,' she said.

We waited anxiously until Dad could hold back no longer. 'Can you feel it, doctor?'

Doctor Murray looked up, let go of Lily's wrist, and gave the slightest shake of her head.

Forty-nine

'What now?' asked Dad. Mum had her hand over her mouth and tears were starting to flow down her cheeks, but I was too shocked to cry.

'I'm trying for another pulse,' said the doctor, pressing her fingers on Lily's neck.

We stood there, hardly daring to breathe. I squeezed my eyes shut and felt the blood pounding in my head. The waiting was unbearable.

Then Doctor Murray said, 'There's a pulse. It's a weak one. But Lily is alive.'

The relief was tremendous. We all breathed again and Dad wrapped his arms round Mum, hiding his own tears on her shoulder.

'Could I have a bowl of water and a cloth, Daisy?' asked Doctor Murray. 'I need to clean the wound at the back of Lily's head. We can't have it getting infected, can we?'

I hurried into the kitchen to fetch the water. Once I'd carried it upstairs, I stood by the bed watching every movement the doctor made, imagining I was a nurse. One day, I'll be able to help people, I thought. Just like Doctor Murray was helping us.

The bowl of water soon turned pink with Lily's blood and I had to carry it downstairs. As I poured it away down the sink, I couldn't help thinking of Lily losing all that precious blood and I wanted to cry.

'I've made some tea, Daisy,' called Mrs Bryce who had come down earlier. Thomas had lit the fire in the front room and his mother had put the kettle on. 'Take this up, will you, my love?' she said to me as she poured tea into three cups. I carried them up on a tray and left Doctor Murray talking to Mum and Dad.

It was some time later that the doctor came downstairs.

'How's Lily?' Thomas asked. 'Will she be all right?'

'Well, she's breathing,' said Doctor Murray, putting her medical bag on the settee. 'She'll need to be monitored over the next few days. She has a head injury and they can be difficult.'

'What should we look for, doctor?' I asked, thinking like a nurse.

'With any luck she's going to wake up in the next few hours,' she said. 'Your mother and father are going to stay with her. Keep her still. Don't let her get up. If she's sick or has problems with her eyes, you must come and tell me, Daisy. I live over the top of the surgery so I'm usually there. I'll come round straight away.'

'Right,' I said. 'I'll do that, Doctor Murray.'

She smiled at me, picked up her bag and disappeared into the street.

'That sounds like good news,' said Mrs Bryce. 'I think that little sister of yours will pull through.'

Not long after Doctor Murray had gone, Dad came to the top of the stairs and called down, 'Daisy, come and see. Lily's opened her eyes.'

I raced upstairs and Mum put her finger to her lips as I burst into the bedroom. 'Shh! Quiet, love.'

Lily was lying very still, with a bandage round her head. But her beautiful blue eyes were open and I almost wept with joy at seeing her. I knelt by the bedside and leaned close. 'Hello, Lily,' I whispered. As she looked at me, her lips turned up in the tiniest smile. It wasn't much, but it was enough for now.

Later, Mrs Bryce went home to make a chicken stew for our dinner while Thomas walked all the way to Tuttle Street to tell Great-Aunt Maude what had happened. And I got some thread from Mum's sewing box and started mending Peggy's dress.

That night, we pulled the mattress off Lily's bed and dragged it into Mum's bedroom, dropping in on the floor by the side of the big bed.

'Is it all right if I stay, Florrie?' asked Dad. 'I can sit in that chair.'

'For sure, Patrick. You must stay with Lily,' said Mum. 'Where else would you be?'

Dad smiled and nodded.

'Will you be all right in a chair, Dad?' I asked.

'I'm more than all right, Daisy,' he said. 'I'm with my best girls, aren't I?'

Before I went to bed that night, I went in to see Lily. She was still sleeping but I tucked Peggy under her arm. Slowly, Lily opened her eyes and looked up at me.

'That's nice, Daisy,' she said and pressed the doll to her cheek before her eyelids slid closed again.

When I lay down in my own bed, I couldn't sleep because my head was so full of all the things that had happened that day. Mum and Dad were talking in the next room – the bedroom walls were so thin I could hear every word.

'I'm sorry, Florrie,' Dad said. 'I've not been a good husband and I want to make amends.'

'How will you do that, Patrick?' Mum replied.

'I need to start treating you better. The house has been so empty with you all gone. I shouldn't have cared about what the men in the factory were saying, I should have listened to you and Daisy.'

'But you didn't, Patrick. You talked like you owned us.'

'I know, I know. When I was a lad back in Ireland my da treated my ma no better than a slave. Never a kind word, never a thank you, and a beating whenever he felt like it.'

I could hear the sadness in his voice coming through the walls.

'I always swore I'd never be like him. I watched my

mother work herself into the ground and I swore that I wanted different for my wife and my family. Now I've come to realise that I've turned into my da.'

'It doesn't have to be like that, Patrick,' said Mum.

'You're right,' said Dad. 'But you know, I never understood why you were interested in the suffragettes. Or what they were about. I was scared you wouldn't want to be a wife to me any more if you got mixed up with them and I'd be a laughing stock.'

'I was always a wife to you,' said Mum.

'Well, I've learned a lot these past weeks,' Dad replied. 'And I see you've got some good friends. Honest people who are suffragettes. I don't know why I thought they'd be any different.'

'Doctor Murray's a suffragette too,' said Mum.

'Aye and she's a remarkable woman, Florrie. I didn't know women could be doctors.'

'She's an intelligent woman and she's had a good education,' said Mum. 'And I'm determined our Daisy will have one too.'

'You're right, Florrie. You're right.' Dad paused. 'Did you know I came to the park today hoping you'd be there with the girls? But it was that crowded, I couldn't see you anywhere. So I went and listened to Mr Lansbury.'

'Did you, Patrick? And what did you think?'

'I was impressed by what he said. He made a lot of sense, I thought.'

'He's a clever man,' said Mum. 'But it's the same thing I've been telling you for weeks.'

'I didn't listen to you, Florrie. I'm sorry. I was so worried about what people at the factory would think of your opinions. But I still don't see why you should get to vote when I never have.'

'It'll take time, Patrick. It'll happen one day.'

'You're right,' said Dad. 'I understand now that the suffragettes are trying to make things better for people like us – men and women. Well, I'd like to help. I didn't know men would be welcome.'

'You'd be a great help, Patrick, I'm sure.'

Then Dad said, 'And I'd like us to live as man and wife, if you'd be willing, Florrie.'

When I heard those words I almost burst with happiness. We were going to be together again. Dad wanted to change. I could tell. At last he understood what the suffragettes were all about.

But when Mum said, 'No, Patrick, I can't move back to Tuttle Street.' My stomach sank and my dreams of being a family suddenly vanished. I didn't want to hear any more. I was so afraid they were going to quarrel.

'I know it's been hard, Florrie,' Dad said. 'But . . .'

'It has been hard – but I want to stay here, Patrick.' Mum's voice was firm and determined. 'I think I can make a good living sewing dresses. So many ladies have asked me to make dresses for them and I'd be happy doing that.'

'I'm sure you will, Florrie,' he said. 'That blue dress over there is a real bobby-dazzler. You can be proud of yourself. You've got a real talent.'

There was no sound for a while, until Dad said, 'What if I came and found work round here, do you think we could live as a family again?'

I couldn't hear what Mum said because she started to whisper. But it was a nice whisper. A kind whisper. And I fell asleep that night feeling happier than I'd been for a long, long time.

A NOTE FROM THE AUTHOR

I didn't learn about the suffragettes at school. That's amazing considering that these brave women were instrumental in changing laws to give girls and women like me opportunities they had never had before.

Before the suffragettes came the suffragists, who campaigned for women's right to vote using peaceful means. But when years of promises from Members of Parliament came to nothing, Emmeline Pankhurst (Sylvia's mother) decided it was time for action and the movement we now call the 'suffragettes' was born.

Although *Secret Suffragette* is a work of fiction, I decided to put some real-life people into the story.

You might like to find out more about the people I chose:

Sylvia Pankhurst
Zelie Emerson
Kosher Bill
George Lansbury
Florence Nightingale
Emmeline Pankhurst
Muriel Matters
Jessie Payne

There was no shortage of books for my research.

And there were photographs too, and newspaper reports of meetings, riots and spectacular demonstrations showing how the suffragettes fought the government to gain the vote for women.

My favourite was a report of the daring stunt of two suffragettes climbing up the Monument in London, being arrested and giving false names to the police. Their real names were never discovered. They were arrested but then released. How did they avoid being sent to Holloway Prison like so many suffragettes were? How had they got away with it? This was such a good story that I decided that my character, Daisy, could easily have been one of them. So I tapped happily on my computer and sent her up the Monument. That's the best thing about being a writer. You can make people do anything you want them to do!

Secret Suffragette is set in the years just before the First World War. Many of the events in the book really did happen but I've changed the order of some of them to fit in with the story.

When the First World War began in 1914, Emmeline Pankhurst persuaded the suffragettes to stop their violent activities until the war was over. She organised rallies asking everybody to support the war effort and she convinced the government to help women enter the workforce while men were away fighting. Hundreds of women successfully took over jobs that men believed they couldn't do.

In 1918, a bill was passed giving the vote to all men over 21 and to women over 30 (if they were registered property occupiers). Equal voting rights were not achieved until 1928.

I hope you discover lots of interesting facts about the suffragettes.

Barbara Mitchelhill
January 2019

Billy's Blitz

BARBARA MITCHELHILL

When war breaks out, Billy's dad joins the army and most of his friends are evacuated from Balham, South London. But Billy's mum doesn't believe the bombs will ever fall on them and she refuses to send him and his sister Rose away. But by September 1940, things are getting a lot worse. Hitler has a plan for the destruction of London and soon Billy is caught up in the Blitz: an event so terrifying, it will take every ounce of courage for him to survive in war-torn Balham and keep his family together.

'Exciting, atmospheric ... draws the reader in from the start'
Primary Times

9781783440856

Run Rabbit Run

BARBARA MITCHELHILL

When Lizzie's dad refuses to fight in the Second World War, the police come looking to arrest him. Desperate to stay together, Lizzie and her brother Freddie go on the run with him, hiding from the police in idyllic Whiteway. But when their past catches up with them, they're forced to leave and it becomes more and more difficult to stay together as a family. Will they be able to? And will they ever find a place, like Whiteway, where they will be safe again?

Nominated for the Carnegie Medal

'A well-told story showing that bravery comes in many guises.'
Carousel

9781849392495

A Twist of Fortune

BARBARA MITCHELHILL

Sam Pargeter and his younger brother and sister have always been poor. But, in their tiny house in the country, with Ma and Pa, they were one big happy family. Until Pa goes off to America to seek their fortune and Ma dies. Then the Pargeter children find themselves whisked off to live with a strange aunt and uncle, and are put to work – just like Oliver Twist in their favourite book.

But this is only the start of the twists and turns their lives will take. Sam, Eliza and Alfie make their way all over London and then beyond, in search of their only remaining member of family: a rich grandfather they have never known …

'A vivid, enthralling historical adventure' *Books for Keeps*

9781849395625

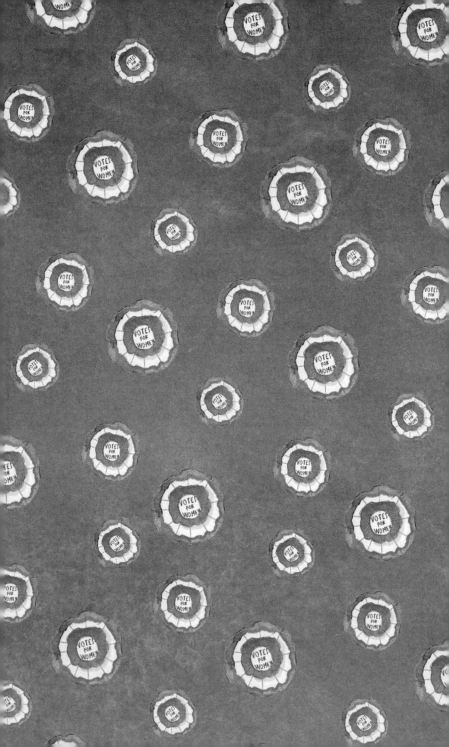